SEAL of Refuge

SEAL of Refuge

Guardians of Refuge, Volume 1

Alyssa Bailey

Published by Desire West Publishing, 2020.

SEAL of Refuge

(Guardians of Refuge Book 1)

Alyssa Bailey

USA Today Bestselling Author\

Guardians of Refuge

SEAL of Refuge

Alesha Campbell loves her island home in Southeast Alaska. Still, after a sudden break up with her egotistical boyfriend, she'd feared she might not find a husband until she met Navy SEAL Zayden Wellesley. The widowed commander extricated her from a sticky situation and stole her heart.

The Navy offers commander Zayden Wellesley the career opportunity of a lifetime. He accepts. On a recon trip to Alaska, he meets the woman he never knew he needed and sets about wooing her. Things are going well over the short trip except for one little snag: He neglected to inform her he had roommates. Now he has returned to Cache island with three surprises.

Zed planned to tell Alli before she found out on her own; however, his roommates had other ideas. And Alli is not happy.

Can Zayden save his career and his budding relationship without upsetting the delicate balance he was already maintaining?

Praise and Awards
Amazon #1 in Historical Romance and Romantic Suspense
&

USA TODAY BESTSELLING AUTHOR
ALYSSA BAILEY

WHAT OTHERS ARE SAYING about Alyssa Bailey

"Alyssa is an amazing author who captures the reader from the very beginning, holding them until the end and making them crave more. Can't wait for her next book!!!" –

~ Bhanington reviewer for Booksprout "The O'Connors Series"

I loved this second book in the Clearwater ranch series. You don't need to have read book one to enjoy this book. Sawyer is in love with Camille. Unfortunately, circumstances worked against them and they were separated from each other. Camille comes back home with her children and they get back together. This is the epitome of an Alyssa Bailey book. There is a strong male character and there is an old fashioned feel to their relationship. I loved this story and I can't wait for the next book. I give this an enthusiastic 5*.

~Marybeth Amazon Reviewer

"THIS IS THE FIRST BOOK I've read by this author and I absolutely loved it. Has a great storyline that you can get right into from the very beginning and I got so engrossed with this book that I lost some sleep as I didn't want to miss anything at all. I especially liked and loved the characters in this book, they really made the story in my opinion... The author has done such a fantastic job with this book and I will definitely be coming back for future books in the future especially this series. I would definitely recommend this book to everyone."

~ Carrie-Ann Amazon Reviewer "Safe and Secure Series"

"I love this series and couldn't put any of them down before the ending. Fabulous read!!!

~Sunny- reviewer for Booksprout "The O'Connors Series"

Acknowledgment

Alaska is the setting for this book, where an estimated 1 in 10 citizens are veterans. I am proud of that fact. My husband, Army Retired, and two of my children have served proudly. I also remember that their families serve as well, sometimes supporting in the wings, sometimes at the head of the line. The sacrifices are many, but we are a tough breed.

To all those who have been willing to make the ultimate sacrifice to protect the freedoms and way of life we enjoy, I thank you. To those who have answered the call and have made the ultimate sacrifice, I am in your debt. And for all those who understand what it means to say,

"I will not fail."

Thank you.

Prologue

"What do you mean you have to quit this week? Like tomorrow?"

Commander Zayden "Zed" Wellesley rubbed the back of his neck in aggravation. Not for the first time, Zed wondered why the good Lord would give him three incredible children but take their mother away long before she raised them. He was an elite member of the military, a Navy SEAL. It was typical to divorce at least once and often more times before suffering the loss of a spouse. For seven years, he'd been one of the lucky ones.

The military had trained him to respond in every contingency, except the loss of his wife. There was no training to prepare you for that disaster, no SOP manual written to address it. Likely because there were no standard operating procedures when handling the inexplicable pain that followed that devastating loss.

"Yes. I'm sorry, but I've been accepted to John Hopkins University for the nuclear biology program. Someone dropped out. I can use my scholarships, making it affordable, but I have less than two weeks to get it all together, sir."

"Right, meaning you'll be here tomorrow, and that's it. Well, we need more scientists, so you'd better go." He released an exaggerated sigh before giving her a big smile. "All right, kid-

4

do, do you have any suggestions for a replacement?" he asked as he raked fingers through his military-style hair, glancing around his semi-clean kitchen trying to think.

"I wanted to tell you first, sir, then I would check for a replacement."

"Okay, thanks and congratulations!"

"Thank you, sir. And... I'm sorry."

"You're a smart young lady. Grab the brass ring when you can. Life is short and changes quickly."

Zed rubbed his face in frustration before picking up the phone in his office to dial the base, waiting for his friend and co-worker to answer.

"Mason."

"Hey, it's me, Zed. What's your Commander calendar look like today?"

"Sounds serious."

"Could be, but not urgent."

Zed ran his hand through his hair. He reached down and rubbed his neck while he waited for his friend to respond and that irritated him. Tells that he'd all but eradicated until three years ago taunted him at the most inopportune times. He'd let his guard down to deal with more immediate issues. In the field, he rarely faced an issue he didn't have an immediate contingency plan for, but at home, that was another matter entirely. He brought his hand to his side in a jerky motion. *At this rate, I'll be bald with a raw neck.*

Zed listened to the telltale sounds of his long-time friend, Commander Ryder Mason, as he tapped on the computer keys. He was likely opening the appointment calendar their shared aide sent him every morning. "Good til two. Let's grab some chow." He paused, "unless it's classified?"

"It's personal, tied to work. My personal life ceased to be classified the moment I had to parent my family alone. I'm starving."

Over large steaks and baked potatoes with the requisite salad, they talked.

"I must have a curse or something. Fifth sitter in a year. I thought I was doing well. I kept Frances for almost six months. Don't get me wrong; I'm glad she got into the program she wanted. She'll call around, try to find at least a substitute for a while."

"Yeah, well, maybe that'll work until you're assigned another team, and you're gone for a week, a month, or more. With part of you worried about the kids here and part on the mission," Mason shrugged.

"I know it's not ideal, but what am I to do?"

"Command knows that I've been thinking about you a lot lately. I've concluded that you and your family need something different. You need more than existing here."

"I'm not leaving the military. I've got fourteen good years in, and I'm not throwing that away."

"No, that isn't what I'm saying at all. I wouldn't support that decision, none of us would. But you need something else. Something that meets your need to serve, that puts your skills to work and keeps you in with the Spec Ops."

"Sounds like my dream job."

"Well, listen. There's a newly created assignment coming open for multi-service training in cold water, cold climate, rough terrain operations. You know, neutralizing the home-grown threats, only magnified."

Zed laughed. "Where is it, the South Pole? Newfoundland?"

"Cute, I wouldn't have had any trouble sending your ass to one of those places, but I'm not sending the kids that far from their support system. It's a training and testing center. You know, your standard submarine, sonar, environmental research station. I hear even marine biologists come by to do research there. But that's not all." He took a bite of salad.

"I'm listening. So, where is it located?"

"It's on a small island in Southeast Alaska. The Navy is already there, reservists, too. We're expanding the base to include another building. That will be for you. The exercises will be off-site, but the instructional foundation will be on site. You'll administer everything from there. The powers that be have increased their presence at the base to include cold climate specialized training. It might just be the ticket for you. Get you out of the rat race." Mason gulped his iced tea.

"Why, exactly, is there the need for this new training center? You'd think we had enough."

"Consolidation of resources. Due to the changing of the guard in the world today, and the more stalwart the opposition has become, there seems to be a greater need for stronger, smarter elite forces. They, the federal and local governments, want to expand the island's uses, and they've created this new arc. It's a response to consolidation mandates. They're creating a training segment for all U.S. Forces. It will be for all services, to include the Air Force."

Both men gave an appropriate grunt of good-natured rivalry. Mason drew a special target on the Air Force because his younger brother had chosen that branch of the service to pledge his professional allegiance. Mason contended his brother wasn't satisfied with leaving sibling rivalry in childhood.

"You'd head the new program which would include SEALs, Black Ops, Spec Forces. You name it. If an alphabet government agency wants the training, military or civilian, they must schedule it with you, but we've agreed to accommodate if they co-fund. I've only seen the preliminary numbers, but your budget for this project is impressive. And command would look at putting you on a fast track to your next promotion after the first successful year. And Zed, you'd keep your trident."

Zed leaned back in his chair. Training is off-site, and the site is off the island. That still takes me from the kids too often, this time without family support."

"You won't be doing the actual training except for your staff unless you want to do a session here and there. Your job will be to set up the program, make the connections, implement, oversee it, and report on it. It'll be your signature they will look for on the paperwork and your ass on the line if things don't fly. Your actual job site would be an island a few miles from home, meaning you would commute by boat. I guess you could swim to work to keep up on your PT. You can select your instructors and support team. Since it's a multi-service training center allowing you to pick from all branches of the military as staff, the field is wide open. We want the best as much as you do, so we have some select members to add to your selection choices."

"Just how intense is this training supposed to be?"

"Part of that will be up to you and the needs of those coming to you. Remember that this is elite training for elite operatives to work specifically on domestic soil. We intend funneling more to you as we see the success rates."

"I assume my new team would need to be well trained already to the more restrictive rules when working within homeland borders."

"Yes, within reason. We don't want conventional tactics here, Zed. In a way, we're looking at sanctioned mercenary work, but we will deny it if asked. Each agency and military service will create their parameters themselves, but the training will be by the book. If they step outside those guidelines, it won't come back to scorch your ass."

Zed snorted a chuckle. "SOP, then."

"That's another thing. You're going to have to write your standards of operation, so pick a capable clerk. How many levels are we going? I'll need a ceiling, and other parameters outlined."

"Sure. You'll have to run your team through the course, and they'll need to meet your expectations. My advice is to choose those who could take the lead on specific segments as your SEAL teams did. Then snag a team leader like an earlier you. One with too much ambition and training for his own good." Zed laughed at Ryder's good-natured jab. "Then mold them for what you want. Experience works only if they're willing to adjust to your type of commanding style."

"I hear what you're saying. I have a few men in mind and a woman whom I worked with recently.

"This movement has to do with Domestic Search and Rescue on the water, in the air, and in the surrounding mountains and rainforest, high altitude, severe cold weather training for anything from domestic terrorism to kidnapping to natural disasters here and in Canada. We're setting up a counterpart in the deep South that will take on the lower regions, including Mexico, if they want it. The southern group has such a hot border; it will take up most of their energies. The actual division of work will be ironed out before you train your first group. It's what you've had and more, but with the added intensity of focusing on things we deal with here on our soil."

"What about those mercenary rescue groups that have surfaced from ex-military?" asked Zed.

"I imagine it'll vary according to what the desired result is, but you'll work that out. There's a component for authorized civilians. There is a group out of the Midwest and one Bellingham region that has taken on both international and domestic disturbances. The Feds seem to love them."

"All prior military?"

"Mostly."

The men took a moment to digest not only lunch but their thoughts. Ryder continued. "The whole state is your playground, and we would make this permanent. Hell, if you need to fill out your numbers, we might even let in the Rangers and the Raiders." The men laughed, knowing they each had good friends in those elite forces.

Zed leaned back in his seat. "It's a lot to think about."

"It's unannounced at this point. You wouldn't have to fight for it. I have it on good authority that you would be an easy choice. You could make this assignment your own and raise the kids in a relatively crime-free environment. I hear that there are more women now than there used to be."

"What, not ten men competing for one woman any longer? So, the sport is gone out of mating in untamed Alaska now?"

Ryder shook his head and chuckled. "Yeah, all right, but this could be the right choice for many reasons."

"Am I that pathetic raising the kids alone?" Zayden's uncertainty was evident in the question, if not the tone.

"Are you kidding me? Your adaptive skills and the way you've taken over command of the home front is astounding. Just as I would expect one of my SEAL team leaders to handle it, but I know it's harder than a day in the field."

"But..."

"But being an elite operative is a lonely job, Zed and not one for raising a family alone. Your kids are still young. They need a mother, and its time you had a companion, a sounding board, a lover. Someone to kick you where you need it when you do too much or are too hard on yourself. You need a wife. You might find one there. A slower pace allows you to notice the environment, and I don't mean to conquer it as hostile terrain."

"You're right. I miss all those things and more." Zed played with the thoroughly gnawed bone on his plate.

"And it's a much smaller community. I know the teams are like family, but the truth is, you need that and more. You need a team *and* a wife. Those men will always be part of your family, hell, you'll probably have a good amount of them join you as training instructors. If an injury or other issues don't get them, when they get to where you are now, at a crossroads, I'm sure they will look at joining you. Your new team, the one you hand-pick, will be there with you. I anticipate you sifting through guys for a while until the cream has risen to the top. It can start with you."

"How much time do you think I might have to decide?"

"I'd say throw your hat in now, while you're working be-tween the teams because it's the best time to make a change. I'd also advise you to make your decision by Monday because it hits the airways Tuesday. It won't, though, if you notify them you want it."

"All right. I'll think about it."

Chapter One

Mason was right. Things were different now. Hell, everything was different since they'd lost Chrissy. He hadn't checked the car out before she'd gotten in it. The thought crossed his mind, but he'd dismissed it. If he were on a mission, he would have never ignored even a random thought. The insurance company said the car's brake system was faulty. If the recall announcement had gone out when it was slated to, she would likely still be alive. It triggered an immediate recall, but by then, she was gone.

He'd heard what they'd said, but he'd failed her too: his best friend, the mother to his children, his lover. It was his fault because he'd missed the opportunity to be Chrissy's protector, but it would never happen again. He was anal about safety, which made his nine-year-old daughter Katrina roll her eyes sometimes but made him the right candidate for this job. He kept his old teams safe, his family protected, and he would train the new teams to exhibit those same characteristics.

Since the accident, he was extra diligent with the children's welfare. How could he not be when he had precious lives to guard? No, he'd do his damn job for his teams, in service to his country, and most importantly, at home. He would never come up short again, never be found wanting in his obligations.

Zed and his various teams had been to Alaska many times on maneuvers. He'd done a couple of TDY assignments out of there, but that was all farther north. He'd done nothing south of Yakutat. Throughout the afternoon, Zed's inbox filled with emails on the training center. Ryder must have talked to someone as soon as he returned to the office. The program already had a name: Joint Forces Extreme Environment Training Center (JFEETC).

They'd already sent him some suggested team names to make the group immediately cohesive and identifiable. He'd decided on Guardians of Refuge. Much like the unit Guardian Angels, the mission of seeking out and recovering those in harm's way, the Guardians of Refuge would-be protectors of those in mortal danger, within their North American borders by identifying, invading, and destroying the enemy. Those who were authorized could take the name of "Guardian," and add to it their own group's identifier if desired.

Those trained by his Guardians would always defend by being on the offensive. Proactive. That's the way to clear out those who thought the laws of the land didn't apply to them. Zed experienced a deep satisfaction that he would be part of the reason the scumbags got the message that America was cleaning their house. Not identified by ethnicity or religious beliefs but by their deeds. These assholes were dangerous and cunning, but his trained elites would be more so.

While stationed in Southeast Alaska, he would take or send, whichever the case might be, to any part of the state according to what type of training they were there to complete, dictated by what their job was. His permanent team and any trainees would always be available for real-life scenarios, according to emails he had gotten the last few days. The more the plan was made known to him through telephone conferencing over the remainder of the week, the more he was excited to start the process.

On Friday night, he knew the time had all but run out on his decision-making process. It was a long night of weighing pros and cons, something he didn't often need to do when on a mission. Decisions were made without much mental debate, but the weight of his choices for his children caused him to doubt his thinking. He alone was the keeper of their futures.

Zayden got up Saturday morning and looked at himself in the mirror. He'd put off discussing this job potential with Katrina because, well, he wasn't sure what to say. Staring at his face reflected in the mirror, he gave himself a pep talk, also known as chewing his own ass. *It's time to make a command decision.*

"You're thirty-six years old with just over fourteen years in this outfit. If you aren't going to be happy with the desk job, then you better figure this out. You've been given a good opportunity, so what are you going to do with it?" He headed for the kitchen. His eldest daughter walked in as he was reaching for the coffee.

Every time he looked at Katrina, he missed her mother, but after three years, the pain was lessening. Katrina was a true blending of he and Chrissy, but she favored her mother. Zed never intended to remarry, but raising these rug rats alone was difficult. Recently the thought of looking for a spouse had crossed his mind briefly before he discarded it. It crossed his mind again today, and with all the changes, maybe it was time to look at that possibility again.

Steering Katrina to a chair, Zayden took her hand as he sat beside her. Having a heart to heart conversations or sharing his thinking was not his parenting strong suit. He was great at wrestling around, joking, being the disciplinarian, rooting for the home team, and what his son Kade called, "being the boss." All that came naturally. Being delicate, choosing his words for appropriateness had been his wife's forte.

Zayden thought for a moment, considering if he should say anything before he accepted the position but hell, it's her life too. Zayden knew of all his children would affect Kat the most. She was well established in school, had her friends, and then she lost her mother. Where she lived was her security. Her physical location had never changed, unlike everything else in her life. Now he was about to ask her to give up that one solid touchstone and to trust him, a man who had been gone almost half her lifetime to make this good for her. He knew he wouldn't have believed it would be a good thing, not right off. It would bother him if she did accept things without thought, but he hoped she would at least trust him enough to give it a try.

"What's up, dad?"

Zayden snapped out of his head and gave Katrina his full attention. "Well, Kit Kat, I was offered a job I think would work well for us."

Katrina put on her "seriously considering" face, and Zed wanted to wrap her up and keep her from the world, but he knew that was impossible. He stared into her eyes and said, "but the job isn't close."

"But dad, you won't have the team if we leave them." She was too perceptive.

"I will always be a part of them, but you're right. The new team that I will command will be the instructors who also gave up their old positions. We would create a new group. I'd stay home most of the time. You'll get tired of seeing me."

"So, we'd get to see more of you, and you'd still have a team."

"Pretty much."

"What's the catch?" Yep, too smart.

"We would have to move."

Her confusion was clear. "Move? Where? We've never had to do that before. You just always went to wherever you needed to go. We stayed here and waited for you to come back. That's how it's done."

Zayden could hear the alarm in her voice. "I know."

"Is it because mom died?" The waiver in her voice pierced his heart. At times like these, three years was like yesterday.

He reached his hand to pull her in close to him. "Yes, baby. I need to stay nearer to you guys." She wiped her tears with the back of her hand. "What if you got someone to stay with us? Or," she whispered, "Got married?"

"That is something we will decide later, but for now, we all need this. We've tried it the old way without Mom, and it's just too difficult."

His too grown-up nine-year-old nodded. "Where?"

Zed paused before blurting it out. "Alaska."

"Alaska? Like really, Alaska?" Her eyes lit up, and her face was full of the excitement he had hoped to see.

"Yep."

"With polar bears, moose, eagles, and penguins?"

"No penguins."

Again, that confused look that reminded him she was in the third grade. Something he would never have remembered easily if Chrissy were still here. "Huh?"

"That's in the South Pole, not the North Pole."

"Really?" Zayden nodded. "Go figure." She shrugged, accepting that as easily as she dealt with other vagaries of life. "How long do I have?"

Zayden burst out laughing. "I'm not sure what you're asking me, but I can guarantee you this isn't a terminal illness."

"Semantics." Where did she get these words? "What I mean is how long before you have to tell them if you want the job or not?"

Had she been listening to Chrissy and him talk about things so often when she was little that she could sound so damn much like her mom even now?

"I need to tell them by Monday, so we have this weekend to work on it."

"Okay, I'll see what we can do to make it happen."

Zed leaned forward and kissed his daughter on the cheek while trying to keep a serious face.

"Thanks, Kit Kat."

Katrina stood to leave. Zed knew he would be just as worried about her decision as in his.

"Dad?"

"Yeah?"

"Since we're thinking about making changes, we could do with a mom around here."

"I see. I'll look into it." He almost laughed when he wanted to cry. She, no, *they* needed a woman's touch. The twins, Kami and Kade, didn't know what that meant, and Kat probably forgot what that was like as well. But he didn't forget. He missed it every damn day.

"Oh, and dad?"

"What, baby?"

"Please don't call me Kit Kat out of the house or baby." She scrunched her nose in distaste.

"Roger that."

Zayden had to turn around quickly, so his daughter didn't see the big grin that split his face. Yep, she was growing up too fast. While Katrina might have been too mature for her age, the twins had no issue in that regard when they were presented with the watered-down version. They had other things on their minds.

"Daddy, can we eat mud?" asked Kami.

"Nope, not on the USDA list of healthy foods."

"I told you, Kade."

"Well, it won't hurt you," responded her five-year-old twin brother Kaden.

"Not strictly true, buddy. Your body isn't prepared to digest dirt and little rocks. Besides, the bacteria the water had that created the mud is nasty. Not a good idea."

He neglected to tell them he had eaten plenty of mud in his lifetime and not all as a kid. That info was not necessary to the conversation. Zayden treated his kids like his team, each with intelligence and strengths that he learned to capitalize on as needed. It worked out well in both worlds.

"Daddy, Kade already ate some."

Zayden stopped for a moment and considered his response. "Well, I would recommend lots of water and stay near your bathroom for a while, kiddo."

"Aww, hellfire and brimstone."

Zayden had cursing all around him at work, so his ears didn't even register or set off his dad alarm, but both girls caught it. Katrina was silent but not Kami.

"Daddy, Kade swear-d-ed." The singsong of triumphant tattling floated through the air.

"Cursed or swore not swear-d-ed," he hoped that that would slow down Kami's snitching. His hope was in vain.

"Okay, Kade cursed-ed."

Zayden held his tongue. He wanted to correct her again but curbed his urge. *Pick your battles*, he reminded himself. He turned to the now shamefaced son he adored.

"Kade Andrew Wellesley. What needs to happen now?"

"Sorry, everyone," he dutifully said before turning back to his dad. "It isn't really a swear." Zayden raised an eyebrow. His team and kids alike knew what that meant. He was not one to stand for excuses.

"Okay, maybe one word was. Sorry, dad."

"Thanks, but now go write me something else appropriate you could have said twenty times."

"But my water and the bathroom," Kade was more distressed over that part than the discipline itself.

"So, go write it in your bathroom. Kami can use Kat's if she needs to go."

Kade lit up at the unique idea and ran off. Discipline shouldn't be that much fun thought Zayden as he began dinner, but kinda cool when it was, though.

All weekend Kat asked one million questions. Some took him by surprise, like, "do we have to carry a gun everywhere for safety?" To a question, that he felt was closer to her heart. "Will there be other kids?"

"People live there, honey. We won't be living on Quartz Island, the island that my office is on. I'll take a boat for a few miles and come home every day."

"But we could, right?"

Zayden shook his head and sighed in exasperation. "Sorry, Kat, we cannot live there. We have to have our own house on the same island others live. That's Cache Island."

She frowned, "Fine."

Sunday night, just when Zed was about to seek her out, she came to him. "I thought it over, and I think we should go."

He reached out and hugged her tight. He knew how hard it was for her to decide. "I agree. So, we do it."

He informed command when he had the right people on the phone the next morning. In two weeks, the assignment was officially his and orders were being cut. It was nice to know he'd been on everyone's shortlist. The timing was right for the teams, command, Zed, and his family.

"This is going to be a great adventure, guys," he assured the children.

"I'm not a guy, and neither is Kat," Kami informed him.

Zed figured that if that's all his youngest was worried about, they would be fine. He looked over at Katrina. She was a trooper. He would try to do what he could to make it easier for her, but it was just one of those things they would have to tough out together.

Mrs. Martin, the housekeeper, declined the adventure of living in Alaska. Her last day was the children's last day at school. As soon as he got his orders, he dropped the kids off at his parents, who would then share them with Chrissy's parents and get them to their final days of school while he finished the move. First, he planned to take a recon trip to his new assignment to check it out.

Zayden woke up the morning of the scouting trip to Alaska with a sense of renewed hope that this move was a good one. He decided that it was time to stop being the widower and become someone open to new relationships and testing the waters for a companion. He'd be openly trying a hook up to get the first event out of the way. With that added goal in mind, he caught a plane to Alaska to do a little reconnaissance.

Chapter Two

Alesha Campbell looked at her friend Jenn as she sat in the bustling café. Jennifer Williams was managing the vibrant social hot spot for the summer. The owner, their college roommate, bought the café, thinking she would marry her boyfriend of four years. The relationship ended badly. Finding she needed to get away, she left for the summer to take stock of her life and to heal.

Alesha, Alli to her friends, knew all about that lost, angry, desperate feeling after being dumped. Two years ago, it had happened to her in an equally dramatic way, but Alli didn't do the world traveler route. She'd bought a house and went back to teaching nursing in the local college, leaving behind the remains of a broken romance and her dream of a professorship. Clean start. She'd grown up in Port Refuge, which meant she'd have to go off-island to find someone she didn't grow up with and when would that happen. Never.

Besides, first, she had to trust again. She'd believed Chad and his promises. It was that betrayal of her trust that hurt the most. Things like he'd always be there for her, her protector, her lover, a partner in life. Right. She'd wasted four years of her existence on that expectation only to find out he wasn't the man she'd thought, far from it. His immaturity and regard for her were highlighted in the way he dumped her. One sentence on a damn social media message at the end of the university's spring break. You'd think he was a student rather than an associate professor.

She'd moved home; he'd stayed. But the residual faith in her ability to pick a man worth his salt was damaged. She questioned her ideology concerning what she wanted in a mate. It undermined her self esteem, and no matter how much self-talk she engaged in, it did not obliterate all that Chad had done to her.

Jenn spoke vehemently. "I told you he was an asshole when you met him. Stop thinking about him. It's been over two years now. Get new blood."

"I *am* over him." Alesha passed a suspicious eye over her friend. "Are you psychic or something? How did you know I was thinking about guys?"

Jenn grinned and shrugged. "Summer, free time, single, who wouldn't be looking for a little entertainment? Why wouldn't you be interested in a hot hookup or two?"

Alli knew her friend was right on both counts, but the total, off-handed rejection of the man she thought was her forever had hurt so much that she wouldn't forget that lesson. When she could finally review the signs, Alli could see she'd lessened her worth to feed his under-developed ego. She'd put Chad on a pedestal, and instead of standing next to him, she allowed him to take the limelight because it fed his ego, which was over-inflated due to his insecurities and immaturity. The pathetic thing was she had been satisfied to stand on the step below to make him happy. It did.

She chided herself. She would love to say she'd run from the next sexy, dominant man who showed his protective mannerism towards her, but God help her, she was a realist, and that type of man drew her like a neodymium magnet. And like those magnets, if not careful, its power would crush her. She wasn't sure she would ever recover a second time.

They enjoyed an abundance of alpha males and females in this part of the world, but now, it would take more than that to turn her head. Much more. It took compassion, heart, intelligence, and it didn't hurt if her dream man had a few muscles. She smiled to herself. He must love more than himself. Oh, and plain common sense. Something that wasn't so 'common' anymore.

Chad hadn't had much of that either. Nor had he any muscles. Alli smiled. He was somewhat emotionally stunted as well, but he had a much higher than average intelligence, which is why she forgave what she thought were idiosyncracies due to his intelligence. They were just another sign he wasn't for her. She had dodged a bullet.

She just needed a good man. Was that too much to ask for? Looking around the little eatery at the clientele, Alli saw no one with whom she would be satisfied. None could meet all her wish list of requirements. Consequently, other than a casual night out, she hadn't found anyone to go out with more than casually. Well, not that turned her head, anyway. Jenn was right. She needed new blood: exciting, adventuresome, new blood. Someone to make her sweat in and out of the covers.

Glancing back to Jennifer, she almost didn't look up when the overhead bell rang. It was a busy day, and the wait staff was earning their pay.

"Hey, there's a lost stud standing in the door of my café."

"You're borrowed café."

"Well, I could borrow this guy and pay the purchase price when I forget to return him." She looked over at her frowning friend. "I'm just looking. Kendall is my main man. He's going home to Montana at the end of the summer. I'm going back with him. But you, on the other hand, don't have a boyfriend and aren't going anywhere."

Alesha gave her the 'thanks for reminding me' look.

"Okay, but you bought a house. Roots. This guy is the one the research center said was coming to set up a training center on the base with them. He's a Navy SEAL here to take a permanent job. That means he needs to put down deep roots too."

"How do you know?"

"Kendall was told he might want a fishing tour and that he is looking for a house. All good signs. And honey, he comes from some spectacular stock. I bet he has a remarkable bloodline. He'd make premium babies." Jenn huffed an exasperated breath when Alesha didn't respond. "Would you just look?" Jennifer said as she stood up to greet the man.

"You have mixed homo sapiens with other species of life. I mean, he isn't a racehorse, or a prize rose. Where did you get your education?"

"Right next to you, hon. I've found the right mix of macho and sex appeal. OMG. Look, will you? Those books weren't kidding about Navy SEALs."

"You and your romances. Fine," Alli grumbled. She begrudgingly shifted to get a better view. "And how do you know he's a......"

She stared into the eyes of the most incredible man she'd ever had the pleasure of gawking over. At least six feet, the man's build was solid, centered, balanced. If she could see under those clothes, she'd lay odds she'd find a cluster of mighty fine muscles. It wasn't just that. Loggers, fishermen and all other outdoorsmen lived here. Most looked fit, even boasting more visual muscles than this man, but no, it was the piercing darkness of his eyes and his presence that held her attention.

He returned her gaze with a serious expression. Not moving, he stood assessing her, giving her a half nod before dropping the connection. Watching as he scanned the busy café, she could tell this man knew who he was; owned it. He looked as though every move was calculated, purposeful, yet executed with a type of elegance. No vicarious living for him. This man participated in life. Showed confidence. Alli watched as he frowned as though trying to process the room, perusing the clientele intently. She shook her head slightly before catching herself.

This room housed what was typical Southeast Alaska in the summer. Fishermen, loggers, tourists, shop owners, and artists abounded. Jeans, tee shirts and flannels, rubber boots and rain gear were the order of the day. Many even boated home daily. The uniqueness wasn't only the lifestyle, but the type of personality which abounded here. Alli had always found the locals to be robust in every way. Experiencing an irrational annoyance that the newcomer might have found her little island community deficient and horrified that she still found him worthy of her time, Alli tried to turn away, but the draw was too strong. How arrogant of him to pass judgment so soon. Her phone's incessant ringing interrupted her thoughts.

"Hello? Can you hold on a moment?"

He continued to watch Alli as Jenn made her way in his direction. Immediate annoyance at her irrational response to the man, caused Alesha to drop her gaze, trying to control her suddenly unrestrained libido. Her clit throbbed, and her inner vaginal muscles clenched. That hadn't happened in a good handful of years. Not even with Chad. She forced her attention back to the phone call.

"Hey, sorry about that, Craig. Tonight? Well..."

She took another look at the man smiling warmly at Jenn, extending his greeting to the couple she had just introduced him. Alli hated he affected her so much but excited to feel arousal again. "I'm not... sure... I'll have dinner with you. Just dinner," She admonished before tuning out the rest of the conversation. "Okay, I'll meet you at Gregorio's at seven."

Did Craig say party? Well, if he did, she would not go. As it was, she'd need a shower after dinner. Craig Harlow was a resort developer who had done well for himself, but he was an underhanded creep. As soon as she hung up, she nearly kicked her own butt. She didn't know why she'd finally accepted an invitation from the man. Not true. Deep down inside her lonely depths, she wanted to make sure she didn't give the impression she was missing out on life. Well, a love life, anyway.

Alli sought the newcomer's face again from under her eyelashes and realized he'd moved close enough she could see his brown eyes that seemed to grow darker as she bit then licked her lips. She tried to give him the stink eye, and he winked. Winked! She flushed. Her own body was a complete traitor. She should be infuriated at the familiarity; however, he intrigued her. She could see now that he was observant and cautious of his surroundings, not judging people, just situations. His military training was likely responsible for that habit. She had misjudged him already.

She needed to regain control and get out of there before she made a fool of herself by drooling or something. Besides, she had a date tonight, right? Satisfied she'd found a viable excuse for a quick exit, should they press her to offer one, she waived to Jenn intent on leaving. That persistent woman, now questionably called her friend, followed the man who was melting Alesha's panties as he approached her.

He wasn't merely walking. There was a lethal element to his gait. It was panther-like, with determined intent, but with an unconscious grace few men possessed. She was mesmerized. Alli had tried to communicate a lack of interest by returning his smile with a frown. His response was to watch her intently. He didn't seem to have gotten the message, but she couldn't imagine anything getting past this man unnoticed. Maybe she didn't communicate her mock indifference well, but she thought it was likely he was as interested in her as she was in him. He continued to stare, and Jennifer was barring her retreat.

"Alli wait up. I want to introduce you to Commander Zayden Wellesley. Zayden, Alesha Campbell, a lifelong resident and nurse extraordinaire. Zayden is the guy who will head that training center over on Quartz Island."

"Hello, Commander. Nice to meet you."

Her vague smile was automatic as she listened to the introduction, shaking his offered hand, and tried without success to suppress a tremor when he retained it a little longer than expected, cocooning it in the heat of both of his stronger ones. The effect that one touch had on her ability to stand was frightening.

"Zed. Hi, Alesha."

Zayden's molten milk chocolate eyes smiled back. Oh, she wanted a replay of that look. She wasn't into chocolate like most women, but she could get into his version. His gaze seemed to envelop her in sweet seduction.

"He's here to scope the place out and look for a house. He'll go over to Quartz Island as well to check out his new assignment. Since you have free time with the session break, I thought you'd be able to show him around.

"Um, sure, if you'd like." *Way to put me on the spot, Jenn.*

Alli knew what Jennifer was doing, and she loved her for it even though it was embarrassing. She hoped Zed didn't catch on. Alli experienced uncertainty in the face of such a specimen, and she hated that he affected her in that way. Spending much alone time with him was out of the question unless self-combustion was the goal. Alli slid her hand out from between his warmer ones. Jenn said he was a Navy SEAL. She figured that also meant divorced at least once. She didn't need more baggage than she already had, even though she hadn't gone on a real date with a real guy in ages. She needed to get out of here before her ovaries began dropping eggs. Commander Wellesley stared a few seconds longer before his hands returned to his sides and stood back, breaking the intensity of their connection. He felt it too, she could tell. Nothing good would come from this. Right?

"I don't want to put you out, but I'd be grateful."

That smile reappeared, and Alli was a goner. His voice was mellow and deep. It was one of those resonating voices that made your girlie bits tingle, and your tummy do somersaults.

"Sure, but I hope you didn't want to start tonight because I have plans."

"I didn't know about your plans," accused Jenn, her voice almost hurt.

"Because I just accepted them, but I'm available tomorrow afternoon and beyond."

"Great–" Zed stopped speaking when Jenn spoke over him.

"Where are you going?" demanded Jennifer.

"Out to dinner, Miss Nosey."

"I see and with whom, may I ask?"

"No, you may not ask." Alli tried to appear too busy to give Jenn a cue to drop her current line of questioning, but if it worked, it wouldn't be Jenn.

The commander took a seat at the table that held Alli's phone, empty lunch plate, and a partially consumed glass of tea, her bag on the seat next to him. Alli looked over at him. When their eyes met, he raised her tea glass to his lips and drank. Damn, that was familiar and sexy as hell. She swallowed hard.

"Fine. Don't tell me. So long as it's not Craig the Creep or someone like him, then it's no big deal."

Alli said nothing and picked up her phone. "Oh, my God, it's him." Jennifer shook her head with firm decisiveness. "Call him back and cancel." Her voice dropped to a whisper. "I recently heard rumors about him, Alli."

"It's just dinner at Gregorio's. In public. I'm driving myself. I've told you who I'm going out with and you can call to check on me. Dinner is at seven, so I should be home by nine. It was your idea."

Now Jenn *was* indignant. "It most certainly was not." Her irritation delivered in a stage whisper.

"You said I don't go out, and I needed to start. So, I started." Alli's voice had dropped to a similarly delivered irritated whisper.

"Can anyone eat at Gregorio's?" His voice was quiet, but oh, so commanding. Alli considered sitting back down to save face when her legs gave out but grabbed the end of the table instead.

Jenn laughed. "Sure, but it's the only place in town you need a reservation."

"Is that the only barrier?"

As Jenn answered him, Alli lifted her hand and waved goodbye to her irritated friend and the sexiest man she'd ever met. Summer had suddenly become unseasonably hot for her part of Alaska.

ZAYDEN KNEW HE'D BEEN staring at her, but Alesha was the most enticing creature he had met in many years. Oh, he'd seen beauty strutting the beaches and streets of Southern California, but there was something about Alesha that took things beyond that. It took a few minutes to bring himself under control again after watching her walk out of the café. She wasn't model thin, which had never interested him. She had softly rounded cushioning in all the right places that gave her hips sway. Not in that exaggerated, pendulum way that women looking to entice did, but in an unconscious, natural way that silently seduced a man. She was a sensual, adorable woman who had apparently not been dating.

Zed hoped she was older than she looked, given his thirty-six years. Since she was an established professional, she would be at least late twenties. He wouldn't care himself, but a woman too young might not be into a ready-made family. Even women his age weren't always ready to start a family, let alone assume one. Zayden understood enough about women to know that asking her age was a landmine event. Even when you knew her well, it might not be enough to embark on any age questions. He'd look for signs.

He tried to focus on Jenn's words, but the way she was scoping him out, he half expected the café owner to come onto him. It was behavior he was used to. He'd learned early in his career how to deflect the advances when he wanted to, but thankfully, Jenn never did more than openly admire his physique. That he could handle. He had the average amount of ego, and it felt good to be appreciated.

The person he wanted to hear more about, however, was Alesha Campbell. She'd appeared as interested in him as he was her, but she'd raced out of the café after they had made an ethereal bond that bordered on the physical. It was like her very essence had immediately bonded with his. Oddly, Zed's protection meter was sounding. He saw Jenn's worried response, and that heightened his concern. Was Alesha flighty, in danger? Though his gut said not, he would have to walk away if she was irresponsible.

Did that unexplainably deep connection with Alesha make him hyper-reactive to her and blinded by the flaws? No, that wasn't who he was. He assessed the world around him clinically when necessary. Miss Campbell was playing with fire for another reason, and as his life had proven to him, he never discounted his gut. Zed had tried to take in his environment more fully but had a hard time looking away from her even when she'd broken the gaze. He could see her attraction was as dramatic as his. It probably frightened her. Yeah, he wanted to learn more about her, and Jenn seemed eager to fill in the blanks.

"She's the best sort of friend, but she's lonely. Too lonely if you ask me. She had a jerk for a boyfriend, but he's long gone," she dismissed the man in a quick air swipe, as though sweeping his memory away. "It did play havoc on her for a while. Now, she's leery of getting another self-involved twit. I tried to tell her brains weren't everything." Jenn sighed. "And now she's gone and taken a date with Craig the Creep. I'm a little worried about her going out with him alone and even more worried about her sudden motivation."

"What do you mean?"

"She just told me she was doing fine without dating."

"Is she in danger?"

"Danger? I wouldn't have said so until a few moments ago. Now, I don't know." Jenn stared at something across the room. "Her last boyfriend was an associate professor, like Alli. I don't go for the academic type, myself." Jenn continued. "Now, brawn and intelligence wouldn't be too bad if they co-existed, but that isn't realistic."

She grinned. "Sorry, present company excepted. My boyfriend, Kendall, is a tour guide. Nothing too difficult to handle." She shook her head. "I get to run the show, usually. But Alli likes to share the lead sometimes. She likes a sweet, macho guy that doesn't need her to stroke his ego. That sounds contradictory, doesn't it? Hypothetically, they would run their own shows professionally, but at home, she'd like a guy who took the lead in the important things."

Zed was pleased to confirm Alesha was not in a relationship, and Jenn was. So, Jenn wasn't checking him out for herself, but it was obvious she was trolling for her friend, whether Miss Campbell wanted her to or not. He could work that angle to see what came of it. He'd have to remember the old adage for loose lips with Jenn. She was friendly and talkative and inadvertently indiscriminate with her information.

Primary on his list had to be his children and their stability, but it was nice to contemplate a woman who might share his relationship philosophy. Personally, his biggest need was less noble than that. He wanted a warm-blooded woman who enjoyed an active sex life and could handle his protective leadership. But permanency was on the mandatory side of the list. He was a single parent now, and unlike his pre-marriage years, playing the field held strict limitations.

Zed indicated the realtor's list. "There is nothing in the way of rentals, so I guess purchasing is my only option with–um, with the length of time I expect to stay. I have a list of a few places. I do like one in particular."

"So not like Coasties who are here for three years, tops."

"In my previous active SEAL life, I rarely moved. This is my first assignment, stateside, not on a team or in training. I was on TDY almost constantly, but never PCS."

"Too many acronyms."

"Sorry." He grinned. "I left on business often but didn't move. This is my first permanent and likely last duty station outside SEAL country."

"Why is that?"

"I plan to make this my retirement station. I'm bringing the elite to this part of the world. By the time I have built this baby up, get her a good reputation, and my buddies are all jumping ship, it'll be time for me to do the same."

"Yeah, so buying makes more sense. Go to this one first. It's secluded, a nice area, and Alesha lives next door."

Zed nodded, but his heart pumped double time. Could it be fate that the house that drew his attention the most was the one next to Miss Campbell? Maybe. He checked his watch.

"Got it. I need to go and get a few things done, get a feel for the community." He stood to leave and then turned back to ask Jenn one last question.

"Can you tell me where this Gregorio's is, and what would it take to get a reservation for seven tonight?"

"Yes! I thought you'd never ask, but I had a good feeling about you. I've already set it up in my name, Jenn Williams. You know, in case I had to go myself to make sure Alli was okay, but you would be so much better. Zed, I'm serious about needing a good, reliable man, but is gun shy of commitment after Chad. But if you are staying," Jenn shrugged and allowed the rest to go unsaid. "Here, let me tell you how to get there."

Chapter Three

From the corner table that Jennifer had procured, Zayden watched the scene before him. He was impressed that the restaurant had a fair clientele on a Thursday night but not packed. The atmosphere was more Mediterranean than strictly Americanized Italian, and he liked that. He'd just taken the seat against the wall when Alesha and her date approached the entrance.

Zed watched them as they waited for their table. She was dressed in business casual, obviously not trying to attract. Interesting. Her companion was in black chinos and a rather too bright, green shirt. Her date seemed pleased to have her accompanying him, more pleased than she. Alli dropped her hand from the crook of his arm and took a half step back in an obvious attempt to distance herself from her over-zealous friend.

Zayden ordered a drink and an appetizer. He'd done plenty of these types of 'cushy' missions following the target to nice places, infiltrating their lives as necessary, and then perform the adjustment. Whatever that entailed for each job. He wouldn't need an exfil to handle tonight's little caper. He'd wait until they left and then follow her home to make sure the over-zealous Craig kept his body parts separate from Alesha's.

Alesha was ill at ease. She appeared to listen to her date's conversation; however, her body language screamed unease.

Zed had already noted she'd removed her hand from her companion's intruding one several times. They had ordered dinner. The service was faster than he'd expected, and they received their dinner soon after his plate arrived. Alesha was handling it well so far, so Zed refrained from making himself known and shaking the man's hand with a little strategic twist.

Zed put down his dinner fork, preparing to intervene after the man took her fork and ate the morsel of food on it. Alesha stood. *Atta girl.* Zed was about to call for his check when Alesha asked the waitress something, and with a nod, the woman handed her another fork. She was staying. *Damn it, Alli.* The woman didn't know when to leave. She put up with too much bullshit. Something he wanted to fix.

This Craig guy was no gentleman. Zed figured he would help him with his manners. He considered following up his rescue with a lesson in personal safety, but something told him Alesha knew exactly what she was accepting tonight. Why had she done it? Was it because of what Jenn had said, she was lonely?

Zed silently approached the couple and heard the next part of the conversation.

"What the hell," stage whispered Alesha. "Would you keep your hands to yourself and just eat your dinner? I should never have said yes."

"Thought you wouldn't mind since we're spending the night together. We'll be sharing more than food later." Craig shrugged and took a bite of his dinner. "You agreed to come out with me, to the most expensive restaurant in town, and the party afterward. That's full disclosure and agreement."

"When Hell freezes over." As Alli pulled her napkin from her lap to toss on the table, his free hand reached out and grabbed her wrist. Craig spoke with a barely subdued snarl. "It's polite to wait until all parties are finished with dinner before you excuse yourself."

A deep voice, full of dangerous, silk overlaid steel, blanketed the table. "Alesha, sweetheart. I'm glad I found you."

He kissed a stunned Alesha full on the lips, gently but with an air of familiarity. Zed's eyebrow raised sharply as he looked pointedly at the restraining hand Craig had on Alesha. Zed reached his hand out in greeting, forcing Craig to put down his fork and release Alli.

"Craig, right?" His handshake was uncomfortably firm. "Sorry, I don't remember your last name. I'm Zayden Wellesley, Commander, U.S. Navy. I'm here to head the new specialized training on Quartz Island."

"Oh, yeah, Alli said something about it. Nice to meet you. Sorry, how do you know Alli?"

"Mutual acquaintances introduced us. The rest is history, as they say. Um, I know it's rude, but I have a few day's leave and thought I'd take Alesha with me. You good with me whisking my girl away?"

Flexing his muscles for effect as he straightened, Zed took Alesha's sweater off the back of her seat and sat her small purse in her hands. He held her sweater up in silent invitation, giving the message that his request was just a formality. Thankfully, she complied without a word, but the relief on her face spoke volumes. He leaned over to shake Craig's hand again but was ignored.

"I'll pick up your dinner tab for the inconvenience."

"Wait. Alli, you accepted my date invitation when you were already with this guy?"

"It was just dinner with a friend, right? I didn't see the harm."

"But I was," he looked at Zayden, who made sure he was imposing in his stance, "I mean, the party and afterward."

"I'm sorry to be leaving you before the end of the meal, but I didn't agree to more than that. Let me cover the check. It's my fault." Alesha said.

"No one is paying the damn check but me. Just go, Alli. Go with your 'squid.'"

"Actually, it's SEAL, but squid will do. Good night, Craig."

Zed placed his hand in the small of her back to send a strong message, and he was relieved Alesha didn't challenge him. Zed didn't know why he was drawn to this woman, but there was no denying the attraction. She seemed to understand that he was helping her out of a sticky situation that could go so much worse the longer she stayed–or was forced to stay.

He wondered if the initial connection he felt with Alesha could be real. His gut had never steered him wrong, and it was saying she was ripe for the picking if he was interested. He was more than interested; he was captivated. He'd first wondered if he could just check her out this weekend. Do the single bit for the few days he'd be here. As every SEAL knew, often, his first plan was never the plan that won the day, it was adapted to meet the situation presented to reach the final goal. He'd already begun modifications.

He should be upfront with her before they did anything else, especially before he took it any further, but he held back for some reason. The mantle of his responsibility slid back over his shoulders, causing a readjustment in how he approached this. His personal and professional motto, 'safety first, protection always,' was unconsciously extended to Alesha as soon as he'd laid eyes on her. He was in serious trouble.

CRAIG HARLOW WAS A waste of air. Alli couldn't believe that Craig acted such a jerk, and he didn't seem to mind that everyone in Gregorio's could see him. She'd had enough of standing behind egotistical men to tolerate his behavior for much longer. Her ire morphed to fear when Craig had grabbed her wrist. Alli wasn't helpless by any means, especially in public, but she had read the texts Jenn sent her just after arriving at the restaurant. In her mannered mind, once Craig had seen her, it was too late to leave. Bad choice.

The texts said that Craig had been aggressive to the point of assault several weeks earlier. She wondered if it had been Jenn who'd sent in the Navy to protect her. It would be just like her.

That same deep silken voice, now with a hint of gravel, sounded in her ear. "You okay, Alesha? Did he hurt you?"

Her heart melted as his warm breath rolled over her cheek, causing her to close her eyelids in pleasure. His concern and barely concealed anger confused her. They'd only met. She realized he was waiting for an answer and forced herself to break the spell enough to speak.

"No, but I don't mind saying I was startled when he grabbed my wrist."

"Saw that. If he'd kept his cool, I'd have let you finish your dinner. As it was..." he shrugged. "Which car is yours?"

"That silver SUV. Thank you for coming to my rescue, even if I didn't need it. I'm glad to have an escort out of there. I think he might have caused a scene."

"You need a keeper." He nodded at the door. "Climb in. Next time listen to your friend and don't make dates with people you know you shouldn't. And stay far away from that asshat. You okay to drive?"

"Of course. Bossy much?"

He ignored her. "You wouldn't be lying to me, would you?"

She suddenly found the conversation funny. Her chuckle brought a smile to Zed's face as well. "Yeah, I can drive, and no, I'm not lying. You know, for someone who just met me, you have insinuated yourself into my life awfully fast."

"Does it bother you?" still that same soothing, enticing voice.

"Oddly, no. Should it?"

"Not in the way that your date should have worried you, but I can be dangerous in an entirely different way."

He reached over to buckle her seatbelt. Alli marveled at his ease in taking over like he had the right. He smelled good too, like soap and warm man. What would this take charge, knight in shining armor man taste like? She blushed at her thoughts.

"Umm, yes, I can see that."

Without warning, Alli leaned in to land a kiss on his lips and tried to move back quickly. His response was immediate. His lips came crashing like thundering waves on a stormy sea. Her hands grasped his hard forearms, sliding up to his granite upper arms, looking for some kind of stability. His hands grasped her jaw and slid around to rub her neck, slipping his fingers into her hair, clenching firmly but not painfully. Before she lost all control, he lifted his head.

He dropped his forehead on her for a few seconds, presumably to calm his own responses. Good to know she wasn't the only one affected. "Time to go home, sweetheart. I'm going to stay here to watch that our friend who is standing beside his car and staring at us, understands I'm serious about him leaving you alone."

"How do you..."

He grinned arrogantly, "I'm a SEAL."

She tried not to smile in response but without success. "Of course." She sobered. "Yes, I'll be fine."

That's why he kissed her. Not because he had a burning desire to taste her as she had him. But even a man who is making a point doesn't kiss that way. Surely, he wouldn't have lingered. She tried to turn away and was stopped by his hand, gently touching her cheek.

"And thank you. Um, we shouldn't have done that." She licked her lips, tasting the residual flavors of earthy man.

He groaned. "Oh, sweetheart, now you *are* lying."

"No, it's just that it was unnecessary. I'm sure Craig got the message in the restaurant."

"I'm sure he did too. Now, whether he heeds that message has yet to be seen, but I didn't kiss you to ward him off. I kissed you because I wanted to. Hand me your phone."

"Why?" Alli watched him reach over her to grab her phone, his arm brushing her shirt covering her peaked breasts. He put his number in and then sent a text to his phone.

"Call me when you're ready."

"Ready?"

"You're going to go with me to see houses tomorrow."

"Oh, right. Houses. I have a meeting in the morning."

"I have a site inspection, so it works out perfectly. Good night. Sweet dreams. And Alli," he waited until she made eye contact, "call me when you get home."

Alli drove away as she watched Zed in the rearview mirror saunter back to lean against the driver's side of Craig's car. Craig, idiot that he was, didn't leave in enough time. He was still standing outside his vehicle when Zed walked up. Zed was making sure she had enough time to get to her house, but they lived on an island; Craig knew where she lived. Somehow, she figured that wouldn't make any difference where Zed was concerned. She didn't worry, Craig was a jerk, but he was probably harmless.

She made it home. Alli thought it was sweet of him, but it was unnecessary to call Zed. His training made him overly careful, and it was a nice gesture, but he wouldn't really want her to call him. She sent a quick text.

"Home."

Almost immediately, her phone rang. "I said, call me, sweetheart. That means I need to hear your voice. Anyone can send a text. It doesn't tell me you're not in trouble."

"Overprotective much? I'm fine. I'm home, safe and sound."

"Good, lock your doors and windows."

"All done."

"Set your alarm."

"Don't have one." He grumbled something she couldn't understand, but his frustration could be heard. "And don't need one." She added. "It's safe here."

"Yeah, I can see that after tonight."

She rolled her eyes. "I'm going to bed now. Thank you for taking care of Craig for me. Wait, you did just stall him, right? I mean..."

Zayden sounded like he was going to chuckle, but it soon morphed into something more akin to a growl. "I didn't do anything physical if that is your question. Trust me, I don't intend to meet the police on this visit. That is slated for after I take up residence. I won't say he didn't get a little fear therapy, though."

"Good. Okay. I think. Um, I'll see you tomorrow."

"Good night, sweetheart."

Alli lay in bed, unable to fall asleep. The commander was such a contradiction. He was gentle and kind, and familiar... he called her sweetheart and damn if it didn't make her body tingle all over. On the other hand, he was a force to be reckoned with, demanding but accommodating, and hot in every way except his dealing with trouble. Then he was cool as the proverbial cucumber. She could imagine that man doing all sorts of naughty things to, with, and for her. And her Sahara dry sex life was ready for anything her imagination could cook up. Or his.

Maybe Mr. Sexy SEAL would be ready for a hot hookup weekend? She wasn't that type of girl, but if it got her pink bits some action and it was with a panty-melting representative of the Navy, what could she say? He obviously had standards as he had so ably demonstrated tonight. Alli sighed. She wouldn't do it; however, her dreams didn't appear to get the memo. After waking up the second time during the night, hot and achy for loving, she knew she was in serious trouble.

Chapter Four

Waking up to more surprising sunshine in this temperate rainforest, Zed took it as a good sign. This whole environment was majestic. Tall trees, abundant wildlife everywhere, huge expanses of ocean, waterfalls, and crisp, clean air all enclosed in so many mountains, it took his breath away. He counted that a small miracle because he'd been all over the world and seen all kinds of things. This was pure somehow. The things he'd dreamed of doing with and to Alesha had him waking with a massive woody he'd spent a while in the shower to appease.

He prepared for the day with his mind focused on pursuing Miss Campbell and exploring his attraction. He was confident of success because when a SEAL wanted something, they found a way to get it. The thought made him hypervigilant and excited, like a new mission. Hunger drove him from the room in search of breakfast, envisioning having Alesha instead.

Since the little Coffee Cache from last evening didn't open for food until ten, and he needed to be in the street by then, he found another place with a fisherman's wharf atmosphere and stopped in there. After ordering a breakfast large enough to last him a while, he bought a copy of the thin local paper to read the news for Cache Island, the community of Port Refuge, and surrounding islands.

The turn of the page sent his fork to the floor, clanging as it hit. He automatically bent to retrieve it. Raising without thought, he slammed into none other than the woman who danced sensually in his dreams last night. Startled, he found himself presented with the widened eyes of an equally surprised Alesha Campbell. It had to be providence that she was passing his table. He grinned, mentally seeing her naked, and compliant in his bed, hot and bothered and sexy as hell.

"Oh, hey. Sorry about the sudden entry. Dropped my fork." He held it up.

Her face turned the most adorable pink, and she immediately broke eye contact. That wouldn't do. "Why don't you have a seat and join me?" *On my lap, if you'd prefer.* Zed tried to perform an about-face mentally. He'd already lost his head at nine a.m.

Alesha smiled and nodded. "For just a minute." She tossed her bag beside her on the bench seat and turned to look longingly at his coffee cup.

"Tea, right?"

She appeared puzzled. "How did you know?"

"Your lunch yesterday." Her smile warmed.

He realized right then and there that he'd do anything for more of her sweet, engaging smiles and a chance to kiss those lips again.

"Yes, but that was iced."

He shrugged. "You had a teabag in your purse yesterday, too."

"Observant if a little creepy."

For the first time since Chrissy, he noticed the honesty in a woman's manner. Alesha seemed like an open book. What he wouldn't do to get between her pages. When had his thoughts gone so lustfully juvenile?

"You have a good memory."

"Always when it's something worth remembering."

Another wave of red flushed her cheeks. "Thank you. Um, how're you doing this morning? You found breakfast, I see. Reindeer sausage? One of my favorites." He smiled at the familiarity as she reached across the table and snagged one of his strawberries.

"Yep, that's something I'm good at, finding food. Want a bite, or can I order you something else besides tea?"

She smiled as a blush colored her cheeks. Shook her head. "I'm good. I do like coffee but in the evening. Odd, I know, but that's how I like it." She shrugged. "And I love strawberries."

Zed raised his hand to hail his server as he filed another tidbit about Alesha way in his retrievable file.

"So, what's on your agenda this morning besides tea and your meeting?" asked Zed. He was struck suddenly at how domestic this was and how much he loved it.

"I'm on my way to finish my errands before the eleven o'clock meeting at the café. We're brainstorming for the Fourth of July parade over lunch. It's a huge holiday here." She folded the napkin in front of her. "So, finding everything you need?"

Zed noticed she didn't mention last night at all. He wouldn't either for now. There was time for that later.

"Well, yes and no."

Zed gave his dirty fork to the waitress, ordered tea, and accepted more coffee. The female server smiled broadly at him as she quickly brought a new fork. Zed noticed her extended glance, the unspoken offer and worried for a moment that both women thought he was flirting. He returned a distracted smile and thanked the cute server before resuming his conversation with Alesha, effectively rebuffing her.

"I have things to do until the early afternoon, but then I'm all yours if you're free."

"Yep, that works for me. When do you want to meet?"

"Thirteen hundred at the café?"

Alesha laughed. "Is that like when the little kids in the clinic tell me it's thirteen o'clock?"

"Exactly." *A sense of humor, good.* You needed that with kids.

She grinned. "Got it."

They chatted easily as Zed watched her finish her tea.

"Well, then I'll see you at the café in a few hours."

She stood and glanced at Zed as she reached for her wallet. He gave her a slight negative head shake, and she returned it, her hand only grasping her keys. She blushed when he smiled at her, causing the blood to race south. He'd had some pretty exotic and powerful rushes in his life, but Alesha was a different sort of high.

Zed watched as she walked out the diner door wearing the sweetest smile and taking the softest swaying backside he'd seen in a good long while with her. Envisioning his hands moving up and down the curvy planes of her hips and bottom brought his cock to half-mast and rising. He'd need to learn how to temper that physical heralding of her presence, or he would be forever hiding behind things. What a good problem that was to have.

While he finished breakfast, he reorganized his list into priorities, and the new focus was on Alesha. She might be the real thing. She was certainly captivating him, and his instincts said to give her and them a chance. He always listened to his well-used instincts, but Alesha didn't have the benefit of his experience or familiarity with him. He would just have to convince her.

Zed finished breakfast and picked up his phone. Time to get the next big thing off his list.

"Hello Major Martin, Commander Zayden Wellesley here. I've been assigned as project lead on the new Joint Forces Extreme Environment Training Center." That was a mouth full.

"Commander, good to hear from you, sir. Colonel Chambers isn't here right now. Are you in port?"

"Yes, arrived on a recon yesterday. Thought I'd give a shout and make my way over to you, but I hear I need to coordinate more than my GPS."

The officer on the other end of the line laughed. "Aye, sir, that'd be correct. I have a boat on your side for situations like this. I'll call up the captain and give him the heads up that you're coming. Here's how to get to the dock."

Touring the facility was quick, as the place wasn't big. Zed spent the final hour going over the specs with the lead contractor on the new build for his training center. It was impressive, but he wanted to make sure it had what he needed.

He'd already gone over everything with command in Washington, the liaisons from each contributing military and civilian branches prior to today. Seeing the culmination of that collaboration coming together and speaking to the contractor in person, made this real. Very real. He spent the remainder of the morning visualizing the training and the men he wanted on his team. He made a few calls.

With the site visit off his list, Zayden could relax as he checked his time. Ten minutes early to meet Alesha. Perfect. He looked up at the sky, overcast, but not a typical rainy type of gray. The sun must have decided that it had made a mistake by showing its face two days in a row. There were definite plusses that offset the weather. Mentally prepared to enter the café and meet with Alesha, Zayden yanked the door open and strode in confidently. He almost knocked a woman down, and only his quick reflexes saved her from examining the floor up close and personal.

"I'm so sorry, ma'am... Alesha? Oh, sweetheart, are you hurt?" He ran his hands protectively over her arms, and he visually checked for soundness.

"Um, no, I don't think so." She shivered.

"I frightened you. Damn, you'd better stick with me woman, or I might unknowingly do you real damage. I'm normally more observant, but I seem to have too many things on my mind today."

His heart was racing, and he couldn't seem to break eye contact with her. Alesha was enchanting. Her dark hair was up in what his daughter called a messy bun. He'd never thought them cute until today. Alesha must have done it after she left him this morning. Her smoky blue-gray eyes were sparkling with amused embarrassment; her cheeks were petal pink.

"You didn't hurt me." She appeared uncomfortable and laughed depreciatively as she patted her shapely hip. "I'm made of sturdier stuff and am well padded. I would have only bounced, anyway."

"Excuse me?"

Zed heard his more severe tone, and he felt his left eyebrow arch. He had to dial it down, but he hated when women, even in jest, talked down about themselves. The crap the world tried to sell them about their bodies angered him, and when a woman was insecure enough to buy that nonsense, he felt obligated to disabuse them of that thinking. He understood some were vying for attention, but many more, like Alesha, never noticed they did it. Someone had influenced her thinking.

"I don't see enough padding to have made that an easy landing. There seems to be a perfect amount from my angle. Alesha, you'll soon learn this about me that while boasting isn't often attractive, criticizing yourself will never be well received by me. In fact, your lack of padding would become blazingly obvious if you were mine."

Way to go with your "me Tarzan, you Jane" *routine.* He waited for her to become angry, but her face flushed adorably. Damn, he wanted to touch her again. Her skin was soft on his roughened fingers. He started to reach out and run his finger along her cheek but stayed his hand. Did that not so veiled threat of a spanking turn her on?

"Oh, uh, thanks? I think." Her hand moved aimlessly in a flustered state. She took a deep breath. "Please, call me Alli. Everyone does." Even her frustration was cute. She seemed to have as much trouble looking away as he did. And if her tongue slipped out of those perfectly shaped pink lips one more time, he would have to capture it for safety.

"Do you need lunch, or are you ready to go?"

"Nope had that big breakfast and a snack at the base. I'm good. But do you think I could get a coffee to go?"

"Sure, but you know too much caffeine isn't good for you." She looked up, embarrassed. "Sorry."

"Don't be. Some days that would be me but not today."

"Okay, I'll make a quick bathroom stop while you get Jenn to fill your cup, and I'll meet you outside."

"Sounds good. I'll drive."

"What? No, I know the area."

"Yes, you do, but I need to learn to drive around here, and the gas is on the government. Allow me to be your pilot, and you, my navigator."

After a moment of staring as she grappled with allowing him the control, she nodded. "Okay."

"Good girl," he said as he walked toward the cashier.

Alli stared after him in disbelief.

Good girl?

All morning Alli feared she would spontaneously combust whenever her imagination took over and featured Zayden Wellesley. Now he says two words, and she needed new panties. It's a chauvinistic phrase, isn't it? Good girl. She was an independent, confident woman. Then why did she need to turn on the car's air conditioner?

She was confused about the reasons behind it, but the message her body was giving her was clear. *He's hot and all mine for the afternoon.* If things played out the way she'd like, maybe even longer. Zed made her feel special, and it had been a long time since she'd felt that way with a man. She couldn't be faulted if she lapped it up, could she?

Once Alli agreed to allow him to drive, it was as though she'd given him the go-ahead to take the lead universally. And once her misgivings about relinquishing had passed, it was a delicious feeling. She sat back and navigated. He told her which houses he wanted to see first on his list, and she gave directions. He was a good driver who was courteous to others. She relaxed and watched as he talked to the real estate guru. It was obvious Zayden didn't come unprepared. Yet another thing she liked about him as if she needed more incentive.

"Here is my list of things I'd like in a home."

"Three bedrooms?"

"At least. I anticipate plenty of visits from friends and family. I might need to house the occasional team member or a big wig, so I like lots of room."

"You're not serious about a pool, right?"

Zayden laughed. "No, my... um, a friend wrote that. She was joking. I've trained in Alaska several times, just not in this part of it, and she is a Southern Cal gal. I'm sure she will be happy with the ocean."

Alli's chest tightened. She didn't want to know how close a friend the "she" was. Her mind declared it too close without further information. When the agent moved away, Zayden leaned down and tapped her cheek before speaking.

"Settle, sweetheart. There's no competition. You never have to worry about that. A friend means a friend."

He kissed her cheek before returning his hand to the small of her back and rubbing as he led her in the direction of the realtor who was opening the sliding door to the outside.

"Okay, now we don't often have back porch patios, really, but we have awesome decks. Up off the soggy ground and away from too much wildlife at the door."

"Got it. How high off the ground?"

"Umm... all heights, I guess. Does it matter?"

"Probably not."

Alli chimed in. "If you're worried about bears, we have ways of keeping them off your deck."

"Good." He looked like he was going to say something, but changed his mind.

As they walked through the homes, he casually took her hand or placed his on her back. Sometimes he placed it around her waist while asking her opinion, watching her reactions. It was odd since they weren't buying the home together. It was obvious that the realtor was confused as well. They weren't even a couple, but Alli got the distinct impression he valued that opinion as though he'd considered that possibility in the future.

Maybe they would explore that at some point. Alli wanted to know more about Zayden, understand him. She instinctively knew she would only be in as deep as he allowed. But that was as it should be, she told herself. It was just one afternoon, but she couldn't be diverted from her desire for more, almost sighing and snuggling closer as he slid his right hand to the small of her back once again.

He leaned down to murmur in her ear, "A beach near the house would be nice. Peaceful."

Alli nodded. She understood him because she loved having the ocean practically on her doorstep. He couldn't be this right for her in everyday life, right? He was on his best behavior. It had to be. Men this perfect, didn't exist, especially in her world.

But as the afternoon progressed, she knew he was genuine. This was the man in his raw state, and she wanted more of him. He exuded a natural leadership quality, and even when he didn't know about something, he left you with no misunderstandings about his ability to figure it out. Zayden Wellesley was like a drug; she an emerging addict. He was moving here, so why couldn't she aspire to spend more time with him?

By the way the commander was running his thumb along her pulse spot on her wrist, he understood his effect on her. He smiled each time he sent sensual tremors through her body. Something he regularly did with his warm breath near her ear as he pointed out something he liked and encouraged her to agree. Conversely, he protectively and briskly moved her passed something he didn't like, not accepting any rejection of his decision. Such as when she was about to explore the dark lower floor of an otherwise nice house.

She had walked into the kitchen, which held stairs leading down to a bonus room. When she went ahead of Zed and flipped the light on, a dank, musty smell rose from the lower level. Not to be deterred, she began to walk down the dimly lit staircase. Zayden practically lifted her from the staircase, placing her back in the kitchen and closed the door.

"There's no way this is safe. You're not going down those steps."

"Zed, sometimes it just smells moldy because of being closed up."

"That smell comes from dampness, which leads to rotted steps. You are not going down there."

She'd felt put out, but actually, he was right in one respect. Where there was mold, there was water. That wasn't good. She nodded.

"Thanks, honey."

He dropped a kiss on the top of her head. The gesture was nice. The wetness between her thighs was becoming uncomfortable, but if she feared if she removed her panties, she'd have no barrier, leaving her arousal to roll down her legs. Was that a good or bad thing?

He opened doors, stood between her and a barking dog, and even took his jacket off to place around her shoulders without asking if she were cold when the wind took a sharp upward turn. It didn't take a communications class to tell her what she already knew about Zayden. He flipped her switch, and she did his.

Chapter Five

It was late in the day, and the cruise ships blew their horns, signaling their departure for the day. That left the small community of Port Refuge to enjoy the long summer night. The inhabitants of the island knew that tomorrow, another set of ships would replace today's tourists with more seagoing passengers eager to experience their island's beauty. The pleasant afternoon was made more so by the comforting mixture of the bossy and entertaining Commander Wellesley. His dry sense of humor was hilarious, and his stories, how could anyone *not* like him? Alli had never spent a more enjoyable time with a man before. It added to his sex appeal.

When Zed stopped to use the bathroom, he tried to get her to go inside the retail building that held a handful of stores while he went inside. She said she was fine waiting in the car. Zed seemed to grapple with her decision, ultimately extracting a promise that she would stay in the car. Alli rolled her eyes when he refused to relieve himself until she promised. He engaged the locks and jogged to the shopping complex's entrance.

When friends walked past, she tried to open the door to talk to them, setting off the most annoying sound. Everyone laughed and waited for Zed to disengage the alarm. Without warning, the obnoxious blaring of the car horn stopped nearly as quickly as it had started. The lack of sound was equally as loud as the noise itself.

Within minutes, Zed approached, correction-*stalked,* toward her with a frown, the key fob, and two waffle cones. She exited the car and introduced him to the group, hoping for a diversion. He easily conversed with them as he stood holding two ice cream cones. He'd paid attention and gotten her strawberry instead of chocolate. He was the first male, including her dad, who hadn't made that mistake with her. She reached for the cone, and he held it high.

"I require payment for having to choose a flavor quickly before I could look at all that was available."

"Oh, well, I suppose you can eat them both, then."

He cocked his eyebrow. "Don't think I can't or won't."

"Fine."

He leaned down to accept her kiss, and she kissed his cheek. The commander was so quick. He had turned his head and gotten himself a real one.

"That was naughty," he whispered against her mouth. He kissed her again before straightening and handing the cone to her.

Her face was hot again. The man seemed too good to be true. As they leaned against his rental car, he answered some of the group's questions about his job, the new assignment, and him personally, intently listening as they answered some of his. Zed glanced at Alli as she occasionally licked the ice cream to forestall a melting disaster. She liked that she seemed to distract him. It made it easier to admit he distracted her whenever she had any indication he was near.

Her friends wandered off, leaving Zed and Alli to chat while finishing their cones. Watching him lick the melting confection methodically made her almost groan. She licked her own and was gratified when she got the same reaction. His arm slid around her waist as he made short work of his confection. She was falling for this guy. Hard. He finished his cone and straightened, indicating they were leaving.

Sliding his hand to the small of her back as he led her to the passenger door, she couldn't suppress the shiver that raced up her spine and tingled her skin, prickling it. She tried to finish her cone before getting in, but it was just too big. He grabbed it and the door. His nod indicated she should climb in, and after a few seconds of him standing outside her still open door, she rushed to buckle. He handed her the cone and closed the door. All that without a word. Amazing.

Zed sat in contemplation of something as he buckled his own seatbelt and placed his hands on the steering wheel. "You don't listen well."

She laughed. "You don't talk much."

"I meant when I left you secured in the vehicle."

Still smiling, she answered. "I was visiting, Zed. You don't know this island, but we are a safe community. Besides," she cut her eyes, teasing in her reproach, "you didn't leave me the keys. I couldn't open the window or get out. That was *too* secure."

"I believe that was the point." He smiled and shrugged. "I might have gone a little overboard."

"Might have? It's just as unsafe not to have a way out as to be exposed. We do it my way next time."

Sweeping her gaze wide, she saw her effect on him was more than mental. They stared at each other for a moment, and all else was forgotten as she tumbled into the depths of his warm brown eyes. Alli forced her gaze to drop and tried to calm her quickening breath, except they landed on his prominent erection. Zed picked up the conversation, and she had to think hard to focus on it. She brought her eyes back up, that damn flush finding its way upward again.

"Not totally safe. There were forty-three reports of assault last year."

"Most were domestic violence due to alcohol, and reports don't mean verified, but I'm sure most were."

"Still."

"Can we agree it's better than murders and rapes of which there were none. We've never had a murder recorded and only one rape reported in the last five years."

"Impressive record."

The officer in him showed through because he liked to give orders. The gentleman could be seen in his gentle care of her, and the SEAL was loudest of all in that he was safety conscious to the extreme and protective. She didn't mind hearing him give orders to others. It was kind of sexy, really, but not for her, thanks.

Did he take that commander persona to bed? Probably. She wondered what that would be like. She would be game to try it for kicks, but anywhere else would get a big veto. Now she was acting as though *bed* was a foregone conclusion. It certainly wasn't. Was it? Could it be?

"Do you like your job?"

"I do, but sometimes I need a break. I'll be a mom someday, but right now, it's kind of nice to go home after a long day and have peace and quiet." It wasn't totally true, sometimes it was damned lonely but not always. "I imagine my career will calm down eventually."

Zed was quiet for a while as they drove through town. Alli was sure he wanted to say something but decided not to. That was the third time he'd changed directions.

"Do you want children?" she asked.

"I do. I can't imagine life without them," he said.

They parked on a nearby dock, walking to sit on one of the large bolsters of wood surrounding the dock perimeter. As Alli finished her cone, they watched the floatplanes go up and down over the water. The inlet harbor was much busier than the land it lay beside with floatplanes buzzing and boats of all sizes littering the waterways.

The couple sat in companionable silence. Alli looked at Zed's lips as he gazed off into the distance. She was embarrassed to realize she'd wished he would kiss her again, and instead of that desire lessening, it had fermented to intoxicating levels. Brazen though it was and inadvisable for her libido, once the thought reappeared, she couldn't stop thinking about kissing him and more.

"This is a beautiful place. I'm going to enjoy living here." Zed sighed. "Are you ready?"

She nodded as she accepted his help to stand. When Alli turned toward the car, Zed stepped in front of her, placing his hand on her cheek. "Alesha, I'm going to kiss you now. Not a quick peck but a real, toe-curling kiss. If you don't want me to, say so."

It had taken him all day, but finally, she would get what she wanted. She looked up into his serious face and waited for him to capture her lips with his. He slowly lowered his head, giving her time to halt his advance, but she'd no intention of doing that. She angled her face to receive him. His lips teased hers with little tickler touches before he deepened the kiss.

Alli opened to his tongue as he traced the crease of her lips, inviting more access. He accepted. His hand skimmed her back, resting on her hip. His other hand slipped the nape of her neck, into her hair, using that advantage to pull her into him more securely, and still, he kissed. Finally, Alli pulled away, her lungs ready to burst even though she'd tried to breathe through the kiss, she needed air. He placed his forehead on hers, where they rested until she caught her breath.

"That was something I never thought about when kissing a SEAL."

"What was that?" His finger tracing the outline of her jaw. Dropping a teasing kiss on her nose, he leaned back to watch her face.

"You breathe better than I do. I mean, you can hold your breath longer or…" She shrugged.

He nodded. "We'll work on your technique. You'll get there. You just need to practice, and as the new training commander, I gotcha covered."

She chuckled. "That sounds nice."

Zayden put his arm around her waist as he led her back to the car. "I think so too. Come on, I have one more house to see. I was advised to look at it first; however, I thought it better, under the circumstances, to leave it for last. It's a private sale that I heard about through military personnel living here. I have the keys. We can go without our friendly neighborhood broker."

Zayden plugged the address into the GPS. If Alli wondered why he didn't ask her for the directions, she never said. He'd used her as his guide until now. He figured she might still be in shock over that kiss. Hell, he was still in shock at the connection. Zed had thought it was going to be a 'jump back into the saddle' weekend, but his whole being told him it was so much more.

He wanted her right down to the core of his being. If her return of his kiss and her lingering against his chest was any indication, she was right there with him in attraction. When he pulled into her cul-de-sac, he watched her reaction with his peripheral vision. He shrugged and smiled when she turned her surprised look in his direction.

"I had to make sure that we clicked before I looked. If we didn't get along, it would have been awkward to live next to you for years. So, should I consider this house, or turn around?"

It was adorable the way she was seriously considering it. "I think you should look."

Once again, Zayden pulled out his tablet to make notes, but these notes were for much more than pros and cons, it was for improvements needed. He envisioned the children's bedrooms. Besides the fact that they would have an enticing neighbor, he really did like this house best. It had been lived in by the original owners until their death, and now the family just wanted to sell. The price he could negotiate, but he'd pay the full asking price if it meant he could be next to Alli.

Alesha became animated as the reality settled in, pointing out good features and those the previous owners had said they would have done differently. Zed liked that reaction and her suggestions. She was showing all the things she thought made the house wonderful as she disappeared into the room that he'd decided would be his study/office. He continued taking notes on the tablet, things he would need to upgrade when he heard a gut-wrenching crack, and Alli's muffled words turned into a shriek.

Zed was around the corner and in the doorway of the study before she could make another distressed sound.

"Alesha, don't move!" He commanded as he surveyed the flooring around her and tested its strength before stepping close. His hands secured her in place as he looked at her pained expression.

"I misstepped. I don't know if I can..."

He dropped a kiss on her lips. "I know baby. I should have been more careful. I knew the house hadn't been lived in for a few years."

She tried to move her leg and hissed. "It was no one's fault. Help me out." She tried to move her leg again and grunted.

"Alli, stop, honey. I don't want to hurt you."

"I can't stand here forever." Her aggravation was loud as Zayden bent down.

His words were firm, calm, controlled. "Alesha, listen to me. I'm going to make the opening larger so we can remove your foot. It might sound scary, but that's it, just noise. I won't let you fall."

There was another crack, and her foot released. Suddenly Zed was moving her foot to solid ground, swinging her up into his arms when safe. Zed carried her into the kitchen, placing her on the dusty counter. He reached under his button-down shirt and ripped his tee shirt hem. After cleaning the deep but small cut the best he could without water, he wrapped her leg just above the ankle.

"Best I can do for now. We'll get it cleaned better at your house."

"It's fine, really."

"It isn't bad, I agree, but we must clean it out."

"Fine, fine. I'll clean it later. We need to finish looking at the house."

"I'm checking the floors in the other rooms before you step inside."

"I'll just be more careful." The look he gave her was meant to gain a different response, but Alli was a stubborn one. She ignored him, but before she could slide off the counter, he was between her thighs, spreading them wider to accommodate him.

"Let me take care of you." Her eyes were darkened with emotion, and he could see the little pulse at her throat, fast and strong.

She swallowed and nodded. "Okay."

The kiss he shared was wholly consuming. The woman was bewitching. She needed to learn how to be more observant, but that was fine; he was protective. If this was the way she reacted when he rewarded her for allowing him his particular ways, he was doomed. There was no way he would ever be able to get his fill of her sweetness. Zed's lips tingled when he released her and helped her down from the counter. With a final hug, he stepped back so they could finish wandering through the empty house.

"You probably don't need this much space, though. This place is far and away larger than any of the others on your list. The maintenance would be something to consider."

Zed hesitated before answering with a single shoulder shrug. "I like the seclusion, the beach next door, and the neighbors seem nice." *And I have three children who need space.*

But he didn't want to end this budding relationship by dropping that on her before he'd hooked her. She'd made her thoughts clear on children at this juncture of her life. His SEAL training told him to play the game until you were sure of the win. She obviously liked kids, right? She was a nurse, wasn't that a good indication she would be a natural? Yes, she'd said she liked the peace and quiet, as did he when he got it. The rest, well, he'd get to that soon.

"But you'll be rattling around in this place listening to your own echo."

"Nah. I was serious when I said I bring guys home a lot. Believe me, it will be rare when I'm alone for long." He looked around the front room again and envisioned wrestling on the floor with the kids. They retraced their steps, reviewing the important things. "Okay, I think I have enough to make a good decision." He closed the tablet case and looked at Alli. "Have dinner with me."

"Oh. You don't have to do that, Zayden."

"I know, but I want to have dinner with you. We haven't shared a meal." He used his best entreating face.

She grinned, and out came the tip of her tongue again to trace around those pale pink lips he wanted to kiss to a rosy blush.

"Okay, I'd love to. But I need to pick up my car at the café and since we are here, can I run next door to change clothes?"

"Absolutely. And we need to clean your ankle."

He'd expected resistance, even anticipated it, but she opened her mouth and closed it several times before she nodded.

"Good girl."

Once inside Alli's kitchen, Zed made quick work of cleaning and start-stripping her gash. It wasn't a huge cut, but it did run deep, and he needed to keep it closed.

"Thank you. I'll be quick, and then we can go."

He'd wait forever if, at the end of the wait, Alesha was the prize. It had been a long time since Zed anticipated a meal this much. Longer since he'd needed another person's spark and challenge like he needed Alesha's. His cock ached with his efforts to subdue it when all he wanted to do was press its hardness into her hot, wet sexy bits. How ready would she be if he took her now? Zed shoved that thinking away. Down man. He wandered through her older style house, learning her preferences. Zed appreciated the unusual art she owned, noting her taste was eclectic.

Alli pointed to the wall in front of him. "A friend of mine painted that. She's talented, isn't she?"

"She is." He watched as Alesha walked closer in black jeans and a silvery sapphire shirt that made her gray eyes glow. "This is about as dressed up as I get around here." She was so damn cute. Her gray eyes had blue sparks now, and with that smidgen of blush, her skin seemed to glow.

"Wow, you look incredible. Did you grab your toothbrush and something to wear home tomorrow?"

Alli stared for a moment, obviously thinking about it. He didn't want to scare her away, but he wasn't a kid, and neither was she. He intended to get skin to skin if he could, and she deserved to be told.

"Are you sure?" she asked. Zed saw no hesitation and knew he'd made the right decision.

"Absolutely. You?"

She nodded. "Be right back."

Zed followed behind her. Stepping into her bedroom, he leaned down and kissed her cheek as she pulled out a dresser drawer. When she looked up, he moved to her lips, keeping his kisses light but firm. Offering her the opportunity to back away, stopping his progression, but instead, she turned and leaned into him. Chest to breast, she lifted her hands to his shoulders. He needed no further message.

Zed took possession of her lips hungrily. Sliding her hands around his neck to rifle through his short hair, she wiggled, his libido soared. Alli opened to him, her tongue dueling with his, tangling, clashing, relinquishing the battle. She pulled back, breathless.

He smiled wickedly. "Practice makes perfect."

He took her lips again as he began undressing her. The clothes were alluring, but naked was better. He went in search of the unadorned skin that he'd no doubt would be downright captivating.

ALLI KNEW SHE WAS GOING fast, way too fast for her rational, sensible brain to keep up with, so she did the only logical thing she could do under the circumstances, she quit trying. She gave in to the sensation of Zed's hands on her back, running up and down the length of it. She arched into his exploration of her ass, and then the slow, gentle plumping of her breast as his mouth took her again.

His lovemaking was urgent but gentle. Alli would appreciate it later, but just acknowledging his careful attention made her want to give him more. They were moving, and before she knew it, he was on the bed with her on top, rubbing bodies, tangling tongues, tasting nipples. She was burning up in every way possible.

"Zed, please."

It was all she said, but he flipped her onto her back as his talented hand slid, unerringly through her lower curls to her nerve center. He worried that little button as he leaned down to take her nipple in his mouth. No yanking or harsh tugging, just insistent pressure. He sucked and nestled her pillowy globes as he stripped. He was methodical in his equal attention to her achy, heavy breasts. He moved between her legs, holding them open with his now naked thighs.

Her moves became fevered, her legs went around his waist, opening for him. She was nearly there, and then, pain streaked across her ass cheek, a slap, and a rub. Again. The heat, the sting, the tingle was incredible. Her release was just at her fingertips. She became even more frantic in her clawing need to climax. Then, one more smack on the other cheek. She tensed. All movement stopped except for his strumming of her clit.

He kissed her as the waves of release flowed. Silently, he rolled a condom that appeared out of thin air over his staff before sliding into her mid release, taking what her body longed to give him. His entrance extended that delicious quaking a little longer. His movements were more urgent again, her body feeling the repeat of warmth and tremoring buzz as he continued to touch her, take her.

Unbelievably, she was close again. His hand brushed her clit, and this time the climbing wasn't as slow and anxiously laborious as though her body knew he would get her there. The second time was more languid, less pressing now that the original tension had been broken. The explosion, however, was still fierce. The heavy breathing that had been absent in his kisses was present in his release as he teased the most pleasure out of their crescendos.

Satiated for the moment, Alli relaxed as Zed rolled to her side. When their breathing had returned to normal, Zed pulled Alli to him, allowing her to snuggle in. He absently ran his hand over her glistening, flushed body, lazily caressing her.

"Um, Zed?"

"Hmm?"

"I know this is kind of a bad time to mention this, but I'm starving."

Zed laughed. "Me too. Think it's too late to find food?"

She lifted her head to see the clock. "Nope, but you need to get up."

"I was afraid of that. Five more minutes." He kissed her slowly. "That has got to be one of the fastest, sexiest sessions I've had in a long time."

She pushed on his chest. "Why, thank you, sir, but if we stay here, we won't get up."

"Can't we order a pizza?"

"They don't deliver this far out. You aren't in Kansas anymore, sailor boy."

"I'm going to have to reconsider my offer on that house next door then. That could be a deal breaker." He caught her fist in his gut, which he tightened automatically to stave off the effect.

"Oh, man, your stomach is hard."

"Good. Those workouts are doing their job."

He laughed as he patted her bottom and pushed her to the edge. She groaned but rolled out of bed with Zed right behind her.

Dinner was the most fun he'd had with a woman since Chrissy. He'd wondered if the part of him that enjoyed close female intimacy, or at least the ability to do so, had died with his wife, but Alesha had proven to him that it was just dormant. They spoke easily and across all subject areas. Well, except that he was moving here with three children. He mentioned he needed a housekeeper or at least someone to clean his house several times a week, if possible, hoping that would open the subject. It'd make it easier to slide in the information, but she merely nodded as though it made sense that a bachelor needed someone to clean house.

Zed spoke quietly about Chrissy so that it didn't come as a shock that he had been married. Alli had been sympathetic but appropriate, and she didn't seem to be concerned that he was a widower. However, the burden of keeping the disclosure of his children under wraps weighed heavily on Zed.

He was a Navy officer, and no matter the fallout, unless he was on a mission and lives were at stake, he always stuck to the truth. His future relationship happiness may be at stake, and he didn't want to jeopardize that. He needed to man up, tell Alli what she deserved to know about him, and he would, as soon as there was an opening.

Maybe after another round of sex and cuddling. If he were irresistible...

Chapter Six

Alli opened her eyes and felt a moment of panic before she realized she was with Zed in his hotel room. They had spent the last two-and-a-half days and nights together. He left tomorrow afternoon, and she already missed him. Zed was a generous lover, the best she had ever had in her limited experience, but part of her didn't want to know why he was so talented. She preferred to believe it came naturally, and she had no indication it didn't. He'd return in a few weeks. She had that luscious tummy tingle as she imagined giving and receiving a very gratifying welcoming event.

Alli felt for him in the bed, but the sheets were cold. She wasn't surprised. He'd mentioned he needed to run this morning. She looked at the clock. It was early after the long night they'd had. She couldn't wait to have another one. He was much more motivated to run than she could ever be. He was honest, and she loved that about him. He said what he thought while wording things carefully.

Even when he was being dictatorial, which came into play when he was trying to protect her against some unseen danger, he did it in such a way as to make her feel good about his demands. She had laughed at him, but he would not be deterred unless she was adamant. Then he gave in after explaining why he thought the way he did. It was a nice feeling.

Stretching in a bed that smelled like the man who had vacated it earlier, seemed a decadent luxury. His woodsy scented soap, that he evidently brought with him, a hint of his spicy deodorant, and his own maleness created a heady chemical reaction in her aching bits. She rubbed the tingle and quickly removed her hand. The memory of Zed's words halted the urge to assuage her own need last night or rather this morning.

She replayed last night's conversation in her mind.

"I'll have to pull out my electronic friend," joked Alli to the empty room.

"I don't think so, young lady. Making yourself feel good is not your call, sensually. No personal sexual gratification. While you're with me, I strictly forbid anyone's sexy touch but mine."

She laughed. "I meant when you left."

"Not even then."

She'd huffed her displeasure like a bear warning off an intruder. "But why?"

"I intend on making it my job to keep you satisfied." His hot breath tickled her as he kissed a sensitive spot on her neck.

"But you're leaving soon."

"Looks like you will have to find a distraction. There are other ways I could help you out while I'm gone, but it will need to include me. I won't be gone long, so no flying solo."

"That is unreasonable," she'd complained.

Zayden chuckled. "Possibly, but you will not do it. Anticipation and delaying your gratification will allow us both to enjoy our time together more."

Later, when they were lying in bed cuddling, Zed brought up the subject again. "I'm serious about not finding your own sexual gratification."

"Why?"

"I care about you, Alesha. I want your orgasms to be mine to give. You deserve more than impersonal, motorized action. I want your fireworks to be special, not just as a stress reliever, or to help you go to sleep."

"How do you know I do that?"

He laughed and leaned down to kiss her. "Because that's what men do."

"Oh." She laughed too. "Isn't it a little controlling to ask me to do that?"

"Definitely."

He had admitted to the control issue, and still, she wanted to agree when she told herself she should reject his demands. She wanted to make him happy or at least see if she could do it.

"Okay."

"That's my girl," he whispered as he leaned down to take her lips again, sinking into the kiss this time, making her wiggle and moan. And just like that, her body flushed as more fluid bathed her sensitive bits, making her pussy wet and her breasts tingle. He teased her clit until she came again. She had slept hard after that.

Now she looked over to gaze at the entryway when she heard the snick at the door indicating Zed was back and using his key card to gain entry. She had to roll to the opposite side of the bed to see the door. That was because Zayden had refused to allow her to sleep on the side of the bed closest to the entryway. Zed walked further into the room and smiled as he continued into the bathroom for a towel.

"The tourists are here early."

"Yep, but, on average, they're gone by three-thirty or four. We're far enough out where I am, that I don't have to bother with the chaos unless I come into town or go to where vendors are giving tours."

Zed nodded. "Another selling point. I need a shower, coffee and breakfast, in that order. Come shower with me?"

She wrinkled her nose. "But, you're all sweaty and stuff."

Zed laughed. "Yeah, well, if memory serves, you were sweaty last night and this morning. Come take a shower." He walked closer, "I could make you sweaty again."

"It might be worth it."

Zed laughed. He sat on the edge of the bed and reached to rub his sweaty body on her and dropped a kiss on her nose instead. "Later. Right now, we both need a shower." Zed stood and grabbed her up off the bed, carrying her naked body into the bathroom.

"Mm, you wanna have shower sex?" she tried to sound as alluring as she could while hanging prostrate over his shoulder.

"Nope." He pointed to the tub. "No protection against slipping."

"We could be careful."

"No."

"Zed, are you the only SEAL who is afraid of the water?"

"Cute diversion, but it won't help you. I'm the SEAL who will not risk your safety for a little good time."

"Come on. I'm a big girl, and we'll be careful."

Zed slapped her butt hard enough to raise a sting and placed her feet on the floor before dropping a kiss on her tightened lips.

"Alli, I already said no. It's a hazard. I'll get you, anti-slip guards, in your tub at home, and then we can indulge all you want, but that will be after I return. I take safety seriously, especially when it concerns what's mine." His voice dropped to a rough tone, "that includes lovers. I won't compromise."

He placed another kiss on her nose, but it didn't soften the emotional blow. She showered with Zed but remained quiet, silently stepping out before him. She expected him to apologize, but he didn't. Did she want him to? Not really. He finished showering and dressed while she gathered up her things. Before they left for breakfast, Zed sat her down in one of the room's chairs while he sat opposite her.

"Alli, talk to me." His face showed kindness, his eyes warm, his tone firm.

She wiggled because his demeanor was as sexy as hell. That tone, that look, dammit, she didn't want to be attracted to him right now. She wanted to be irritated, and yet she knew it was juvenile. In a way, she wanted him to address her irrational temper. What was wrong with her? She didn't know, and yet, she couldn't shake the mood, even when she feared he would become frustrated and show her the door.

"About what?" she groused.

He waved his hand expansively. "About this attitude. This cold shoulder, your mood."

"It's nothing. I'm tired. There are a few chores I need to finish at home. Stop by when you're finished with things later." She started to stand, but he grabbed her hand and pulled her snug between his thighs.

"Not happening, young lady. If you don't tell me, I'll have to take a stab at it. You're irritated I turned down shower sex.

I've explained that already." His tone said he wasn't sorry, nor did he intend to explain it again.

"I just wanted to have sex. Nothing fancy. Just a casual fu—"

"Don't say it. Don't you dare say what we did was 'just a casual' anything. I already feel something here. I don't know how far this connection will go, but I'm making love. Sex, yes. Hot, heavy sex, but never anything casual. And we can enjoy making love without putting ourselves in danger in a wet shower. Get me?"

She shrugged, trying unsuccessfully to be nonchalant in the face of his sensible denial. "I guess."

"Oh, sweetheart, consider this. If you're sulking because you didn't get your way, I'm going to paddle that cute ass a beautiful, glowing red. You understand that?"

"Not if I say 'no.' This isn't an old western, and I'm not some wench who needs a man to keep her in line."

But she was having a hard time putting any heat in her words. She felt ridiculous with her pouty responses, but dammit, she felt petulant and turned on. The two feelings were difficult to reconcile. Those were some of the best orgasms she'd ever had. His bottom play, whether it was kneading her ass or rubbing the area near her backdoor entrance or even an occasional swat. It all turned her on more than she would have ever believed.

"Yes, everything is consensual, but giving orgasms is my choice. Things have to be safe, sweetheart."

Her mouth opened in surprise. Did he really mean that? Alli looked at Zed and decided he meant every word. Whatever happened to Mr. Nice Guy? The reality came crashing in.

This *was* Zayden. It was the part of him that made him good at his job. That confident 'take charge' man underlined everything, creating that protective factor that did it for her. It was why she wanted him to the marrow of her bones. He was honorable, solid, and took no chances with those he cared about. But did that include her? He'd said it did, and she wanted to believe him.

"Honey, I didn't reject you, just the locale. You can't possibly doubt that after the last few days. I'm smitten and getting more serious by the minute. Your safety is important to me, and it should be to you."

That was it exactly. Zed had hit on the real reason she felt this way, and she hadn't been able to identify it. Rejection, she felt rejected when he didn't agree to sex. She was so hypersensitive to a man's acceptance or refusal because of her previous experience, she put up a wall to protect herself. He'd not said she was lacking. It was his reticence. What a cliché.

She was a grown woman, and she felt desperate for his approval, his desire. She had that twinge in her tummy, and parts lower. Again. It was pathetic. She didn't need him or his talented mouth, hands... she groaned. Who was she kidding? But could she deal with his over-protectiveness, his commander attitude and sensual spanking? Did she like it that much? God help her, she did.

"That's not playing fair. You made sense and acted like you cared. How do I fight that?"

He smiled. "Understood. It's no act, though. I do care about you, and I always try to use common sense." He looped his arm around her waist. "Let's go have some breakfast, baby. I'm starved." He patted her bottom firmly when she hesitated.

It was enough to get her moving in the right direction with a smile.

Zed again refused to allow her to pay for breakfast or split the bill. He'd paid for everything, always. Alli made a face.

"I pay for my girl, and that is that."

"But I can pay."

"Understood, but I'm paying."

She shoved her wallet back in her purse. "You're incredibly bossy."

He chuckled. "I find you need it more than others."

"How many others?"

"Alli." His tone said it all. She marveled that she could feel her juices flow. She needed clean panties.

"Fine, I know, SEALS are female magnets. This is just a weekend fling."

He looked at her as they stood outside her car, his demeanor intent. "Alesha, all military seem to find short term bed partners with ease. Especially around bases, but I promise you few women can be the spouse of a SEAL or any member of the military, for that matter. Chrissy excelled at it, but I was lucky. She could handle things on her own and then hand me the reins when I could take them. I didn't look for anyone to take her place, I didn't believe anyone could until I met you."

She was special to him like his wife had been special. That caught Alli off guard. It almost winded her. Time to change the subject while she examined the possible implications of being compared to his wife. It was obvious she'd been the love of his life.

Alli spoke. "As much as I hate to say it, you have your list to finish, I have things to do this morning. Later, we can go out for a boat ride or a walk on the beach. I'll make dinner."

Zed nodded and looped her into his arms. "I get enough of boats, but never enough walks on the beach with a beautiful woman. I do maneuvers or PT on the beach often, but that's business. You don't have to cook for me."

Alli loved that he was always touching her. His hands were on her hair, her arms, her face. His lips and body touching hers when he was close. She could well be on her way to disaster, but her danger meter hadn't gone off, and she was usually a good judge of character. It was Zed's last night in town. She wanted him with her.

"I like to cook." She wantonly rubbed her front against his torso.

He smiled and then gave her a mock stern look. "Imp. Remember, naughty girls are at risk of—"

"Yes, I got it." She gave him an embarrassed smile, trying to turn from his gaze.

He held her hips, reaching behind to squeeze an ass cheek. His stern look gave way to another wink. She felt the release of feminine honey and an increase of heat at the apex of her thighs. She wiggled slightly.

He became all business. "I'll finish the things I have left to do and then come out. Stay out of trouble."

He dropped a hard kiss on her lips. Alli struggled to think through the sensual fog. Her fingers traced the heat he left behind.

"Mmm. Yes." She took a deep breath and laughed depreciatively. "I'll try," she promised before she got in the car and left the parking lot.

As Zed watched Alli drive away, he fought the urge to follow her. Delayed gratification had never been so hard. His responsibilities had always come first, but today he'd have to force himself to prioritize. He called the owners of the house next to Alli's, and after some discussion, made them an offer. It wasn't asking price and explained what had happened with the floor, citing the need for an inspector, but they came to a mutual agreement. He called his bank and got the paperwork going with them. He would soon be the proud owner of a four-bedroom house.

At the end of several hours, Zed closed his tablet and put away his phone. He made copies of the house keys the owners told him to keep, with the intent on leaving one set with Alli for emergencies. He'd just committed to buying a house. The first he'd ever owned. It seemed he was embarking on many firsts, and he looked to the future with eager anticipation. But like all things in his life, hurry and wait was the order of the day. And there was that pesky disclosure he'd yet to make.

Next, he tried to get interviews for help set up with little success. One applicant applied for house cleaning and two for daycare, none of which was even close to appropriate. He doubted any of them were even of employable age, let alone possessing any experience outside of cleaning their bedroom and watching themselves.

The whole time he was asking these two young girls questions, there was a voice in the back of his mind that kept reminding him he hadn't told Alli yet. His gut said it was a mistake. He still had time to slide the information about his children into the conversation this evening, but something told him she wouldn't receive it well. He'd left it too late. No, it would be better if he simply produced his offspring, and let their precociousness save his sorry hide. Cute usually won the day, and his kids were definitely that.

Zed stopped to gather wine, flowers and dessert after buying the children three DVDs on Alaskan wildlife they could replay on their personal players. He had thought it was an extravagance when Chrissy had insisted on getting them even when he had vetoed the idea. She disagreed and bought them. Best idea of the century. It kept them busy for hours after she had passed away, and he was scrambling to find which way was up through his grief and theirs.

The kids would love the baby animals. He wanted them excited to come and look for themselves. Too bad women took more finesse, more planning. Zed knew he couldn't buy Alli's forgiveness with a few trinkets. Alli had been incredible, *was* incredible, but kids took apologies much better than adults. Mentally reviewing his decision, Zed returned to his motel.

He'd have to get back to the airport to turn in the vehicle and catch his flight by noon the next day. The airport was small and easy to maneuver through, so he didn't need much lead time. There were only a few flights south, and it was only a matter of two hours, but he wished he'd planned ahead. For what? Running into the most amazing woman, finding she was as attracted to him as he was to her? That they hit it off like a house afire? It was only a few hours difference. Had he known he would meet a woman like Alli, he would have taken the last plane home. Hell, he'd have planned on bringing her back with him while he finished the out-processing. He manned up and left the flight as it was.

Zed made sure he was set to snatch-n-go the next morning. He'd thought to leave his packed bag in the room, but as he stood to head out, he grabbed it. He knew he'd want every extra minute tomorrow morning. When had he become so indecisive? Since Alesha Campbell, that's when. He wasn't a randy teen, he wanted this woman, permanently. He prayed she was having the same feelings as he was. In fact, he counted on it.

Walking into Alli's place, he again admired the décor of local artists' work. She was just finishing the side dishes when Zed brought in his offerings. Her eyes lit up, but then her lip crooked.

"Thank you for the flowers, but for future reference, I prefer live plants. Cut flowers fade fast, and then you have nothing to show for it or to remember. I like to tend to the plants and think of who gave them to me. It's like a part of them is with me."

"Duly noted. The wine is one I like. I hope you do as well." He shrugged and pointed towards the creamy berry covered cake. "The dessert, well, it's strawberry."

"You're the most observant man and thank you, I do love this. Now, I'll put the fish in the light marinade, and we can go for a short walk. Can't let it marinate for too long. You can check out the neighborhood. Then we'll have lovely king salmon ready for the grill when we return."

Arriving back, fresh from their walk, the ocean breeze still in their nostrils, Alli was content. She stepped into the kitchen to finish cooking dinner. She walked out with two glasses of wine. "Dinner in thirty minutes. Do you have anything you want to do while we wait?"

"Oh, I'm sure we can come up with something," he said as his lips touched hers tenderly. "Strip for me."

She hesitated.

"Alesha."

He watched her shiver in response to his delivery of her name. It seemed to crawl up her toned legs into her belly, her hand immediately rubbing her midsection, likely because of the tingle. He'd wanted to put that ache there, wanted to see his effect on her. Still, she looked at him as though lost in her conflicting thoughts. Zed imagined her confusion with her yielding body and resistant mind. He had no worry she wouldn't figure it out, but he didn't mind helping. He had a few ideas of how to bring her back into the room with him and out of her thoughts about challenging him. Emotions danced over her face. He didn't want her to worry about the feelings. She'd learn to enjoy them, use them to tantalize him and satiate her.

Zed's hand eased around to her bottom, squeezing and massaging, then watched her close her eyes in sensual response as he moved his hand to her perfect breast larger than his hand but just. She began to remove her clothing with deliberate, measured movements, her eyes still closed in arousal. His cock grew, and he wanted to press his need against her, bury himself in her heat, but a gentleman took care of his woman first. He slid his hands under her hair and cradled her head.

"Your hair is like silk." He kissed her lips again. "And your lips... your neck. Mmm..."

All talking ceased as Zed laid her down on the couch while covering her body in light, almost reverent kisses. His hand massaged her breasts, careful to give equal attention when he took the ruched nipples into his mouth. He moved on to worship her belly with its cute pouch of softness and those hips that swayed delicately when she walked, beckoning him to take her no matter where they were.

As though her mind was warring to take over, her hands tried to rebuff his attentions. "Let me love you." She relaxed and moved her hands. "Mmm, pure sweetness." His tongue reappeared as he moved down her body again, down to where her dark, coarser curls covered her sweet moistness. "Open for me, honey."

She sighed as she complied, allowing his stiffened tongue entrance. He lapped at the sweet nectar that would have heralded her arousal if her moans and adorable whimpers hadn't already given her away. Zed rearranged her so he could devour her goodness before concentrating on that sensitive nerve center. He circled and teased her clit, sliding two fingers through her wetness, bringing his cream coated fingers underneath and through her cheeks to put pressure on her tight back entrance.

Zed felt her body tense in the surprise sensation, but she had already given him plenty of indications at how good it would make her feel to have him back there. It was new but not unwelcomed. Slowly sliding his finger in past her ring of muscle, he intensified the pressure on her clit, loving the little moans as her arousal increased.

Soon Alli was wiggling, a movement he had learned signaled she was close to finding her release. Encouraged, Zed sucked her clit in his mouth as she grabbed his hair. He sunk another knuckle length in her dark entrance. She stiffened. Her grip on his hair made his scalp tingle, and he loved the feeling as he brought her to completion. Zayden smiled. Dinner would have to wait because he needed another taste of the appetizer.

That evening, holding a sleeping Alli, Zed brought her in closer. He would miss her mixture of hyacinth and powder scent, her laugh, and yes, even the roll of those expressive eyes when she didn't agree. Hell, he already missed her. She felt right to him. He didn't know how far this budding relationship might go, but he wanted to follow wherever it took them.

Zed watched Alli as she murmured in her sleep and then snuggled into him. The trust she showed him even in sleep boosted his decision to keep her as long as she would stay with him. He determined to earn that trust. Zed checked the clock and decided he couldn't help but take her again. They could both sleep in tomorrow. They would go their separate ways for a time, and then he would have her forever. Was that something he wanted with her? He'd always hated it when he left home knowing he wouldn't put his feet under the table for days, weeks or months. But is that what he wanted with her, to be home most nights and spend most evenings with her? Yes.

Alli had said she would miss him. Even though he'd left more times than he could count, and it was only a short time to wait before he returned, it was equally hard for him. Zed leaned down to kiss her lips, still swollen from their lovemaking, and savored the flavor of falling in love. Zed knew that he was doing just that. If her responses to him were any indication, she was doing the same. It would be damn hard to part from her softness.

The next morning, leaving an adorable, sleepy Alli on her doorstep was as hard as it had ever been leaving Chrissy or the children when he went "down range." He'd loved being an active member of a SEAL team, but now he was glad he was a SEAL doing a different job, building a different team, fighting domestically. It was time, and it felt right. *This* felt right. Alli had silent tears streaming down her face when he'd taken his lips from hers.

He'd almost said the hell with it and had his mother bring the children up to him, but that wouldn't have worked. He had a vehicle to drive up, and other things that made that easy out an impossible choice. What it told him was Alesha Campbell wasn't someone he could say goodbye to on any permanent basis.

"Come with me." The words were out before he could check them.

Alesha smiled sadly and shook her head. "I can't. I have obligations here, and you have things to do before coming. I'll be here waiting."

"Promise?"

"Yes. Be safe and come back soon." Alli gave him a hesitant smile.

Zed heard the tears in her voice. He stepped close to kiss her again, framing her face in his hands. "I will, sweetheart. No unnecessary risks or I'll have to deal with them when I get back."

She gave him a watery laugh. "Promise."

He wanted to shed a few tears himself when he left. These past few days had been the most relaxed and centered time he'd had in the last three years. Engaging in the self-talk he'd become a master at, he headed back to Southern California to complete the move of his family. Zayden did what he always did, focused on the task at hand, this time, intent on returning to the life he was already dreaming about.

Zed arrived in San Diego, ready to complete the move, pick up the kids, and say goodbye to his support group. They would always be there for him, as he would be for them. It wasn't a matter of picking up his *go bag*, walking out the door, and being handed the rest of his gear. This was all on him. He soon discovered that deploying or dropping behind enemy lines to do a snatch-n-go was infinitely easier to orchestrate than moving his family.

During that final week, his schedule was heavy, and there were moments before he fell into an exhausted, dreamless sleep that he wondered how a person did this every few years. At the appointed time, everything on his to-do list for out process-ing, to include cleaners, supervise the movers and finalizing the hundred and one other things necessary to finish the transfer. Finally, he sighed in relief. His checklist was complete.

The tension unfurled in his belly as he left warm beaches, bikinis and loneliness to head north to Alaska, Alli and their future.

Chapter Seven

She missed him terribly. All Alesha could do was think about him as she watched Zayden drive away. She knew he'd be back. He'd bought the house next door, for heaven's sake, but she had no understanding of the military at all. He'd spoken about how it was before, when he was on an active SEAL team doing missions, how it was after his wife had died, and how he expected it to be now. Still, it was difficult to envision.

The rest of the first day and night was hard. She missed his chastising voice, his tender looks, his possessive touches. It was ridiculous that she'd attached to him so much after just a few days. Maybe he was right, they were falling in love, and somehow, instead of the fact horrifying her, she ached for it to be true. To top it off, Craig had called her twice and demanded she pay him back for ditching on the date by going out with him again.

After intermittently crying throughout the day, Alli fell into a deep sleep waking up only to quench her thirst. She needed the extra hours to catch up on what she'd lost while enjoying Zed. Her body already missed his taste on her lips, his musky scent now found only in her bed and his skilled hands. Zayden Wellesley got her like no other man. He worked at seeing her, hearing her, understanding where she was coming from, and she mourned that loss, no matter how short a time he'd be gone.

Jenn came over on day three, post-Zed. "Why're you so sad? I'd be frantic. You only have a short time to freshen up the new house for him, get ready for culture camp, and come up with strategies that will show him you think he's a keeper and that he would be a fool to throw you back into the deep blue sea."

"Oh, my gosh. Culture camp. I'd forgotten all about it. I haven't even gathered the supplies for my craft projects or gotten anything else done. Think it's too late to gather sea asparagus?"

"You're down for the count on this one, aren't you?"

"Jenn, he's perfect. I keep looking for some huge barrier to stop me from falling in love, but there aren't any. I mean, maybe if he had a wife with a family he didn't tell me about and just brought them with him..." she laughed. "But that won't happen, he's a widower."

"Funny, but he said there were no kids or tagalongs?"

"I didn't ask. Why would I? It was personal, too personal to delve into unless he brought it up. I don't know how long he was married, and he is a SEAL, has just left the active teams, so he wasn't home a lot. It makes sense that it was just he and his wife."

"Still." Jen shook her head. "No, you're right, he's single. I mean, Zed is honest, right? And he bought the house right next door. If he were hiding a wife and kids, he would never have done that. You have to warm up the bachelor pad. Make it homey but not too much."

"Except, before left, he told me there would be workers to start the renovations immediately. That's when he forbade me to go inside while they were working on the house. Something about safety."

"So, go when the guys have gone for the day."

"I do, but..."

"But what?"

"I think he threatened me with a spanking if I disobeyed him. Well, if I got into trouble, period."

Jennifer laughed. "Lots of men do that. It's kinda hot, really."

Alli laughed too. "I guess you're right. And the commander likes others to obey his orders."

"Now, what are we going to do to stop Craig from calling you?"

Alli sighed. "I have no idea. He calls two or three times a day saying, I owe him."

Alli found she could fill her days, but in the evenings were torture. She would hear his voice telling her a joke or making her laugh at the funny stories he had. He could have called her, but so far, nothing. He was busy, she told herself during the day. But at night, the doubts came screaming into her mind.

Maybe after he left, he decided it wasn't all he'd thought it was. Maybe he'd changed his mind. It had been fast. A whirlwind romance was the perfect word descriptor. *Don't create scenarios that aren't there. Take him at his word.* He'd be here soon, and they would work things out. Still, a call would have been nice. She dialed his cell number only to hear his voicemail asking her to leave a message. She sighed and left a message.

Besides working on the rooms, she thought about what she could do to welcome him to his new home. The best way to a man's heart is through his stomach. Only she wasn't so sure it was true with Zed. His smooth tight belly was more the way to a woman's heart.

She checked the calendar and frowned. She would be at culture camp the weekend near when he'd arrive. What day he'd get here was still up in the air, but she'd be away. She wouldn't be able to welcome him back. Alli called him again the next morning, but before the call went through, the doorbell rang.

Alli glumly answered it. "Yes?" A smiling florist delivery woman greeted her with a large pot full of flowering plants. "Oh, my, who sent this?" But she knew.

"Alesha Campbell? It's beautiful, isn't it? I believe the card will tell it all. Someone really loves you." She sat the pot on the foyer floor and waved goodbye.

Reaching quickly for the card, Alli almost tore it trying to open the envelope.

It read: "Sweetheart, I've missed you every day since I left. You're in my dreams and in every waking thought. I'll see you soon, but until I do, I hope you enjoy the blossoms, and when you tend them, I hope you think of me. Love, Zed."

She sat on the floor and bawled. Zayden hadn't forgotten her. Now there was a renewed urgency in his return. Alli added, leaving a note of explanation to her preparations list.

Day five, the texts started. Nothing elaborate or exciting, but the fact that he initiated them most days, made her happy.

Zed: Alli, are you staying out of trouble?

Alli: Ha-ha. Usually. Are you packing?

Zed: Yes. Sorry but it's so busy around here these days. Just wanted to touch base.

Zed: I miss you.

Alli: I miss you, too.

Zed: Did you get my delivery?

Alli: Yes, thank you. They're perfect.

Zed: Welcome. Gotta go. Nite sweetheart.

Alli: Night

Workers had started on the house, and the longer they worked, the messier it got. It was proving difficult as there was no keeping up with the debris and sawdust. After speaking with the contractor, he suggested she clean the rooms he wasn't working on, close the doors with a towel at the bottom, there shouldn't be a problem. Zed saw it differently.

Zed: Hey sweetheart.

Alli: Hey. How is your part of the world?

Zed: Good. Really seeing progress. The contractor should be heavy into the repairs, so don't go over there.

Alli: Okay.

Zed: You already have.

Alli: Just a little.

Zed: Well, don't. It isn't safe.

Alli: Zed

Zed: Alesha Campbell, that's a direct order.

Alli: Fine!

Zed: Thank you, baby. I have to go. Miss you!

Alli: Miss you too.

But she hadn't stayed away. How could she? Time was running out before she had to leave. She would simply be careful. They chatted several times a day now that he had most things in motion for his move. Zed updated her where he was in the process communicated in short messages.

Zed: Damn, I miss you.

Alli: I miss you too. What are you doing now?

Zed: I'm working hard to get back to you.

Alli: I know.

Zed: Gotta go. Movers here.

Alli: Okay. Talk soon.

Zed: Soon.

Then finally, the message she was waiting to receive.

Zed: About to start the drive to you.

Alli: How long do you think?

Zed: About a week.

Alli: I should be back, but if I'm not, I will be the next day or so. No cell service for

the next week. Sorry. Camp.

Zed: Understood. Can't wait to hold you.

Alli: Can't wait to be held.

Zed: Gotta head out now.

Alli: See you soon.

When her day to leave arrived, she walked the note and frozen brownies to his house, placing the note on the counter and the chocolate in the fridge to defrost slowly. She left a copy of her house key taped to the note.

IT WAS THE END OF A very taxing week. Zed had spent three long days with his children driving to Bellingham, Washington and stopping every hour, it seemed, for a bathroom run. He'd thought the hard part of the trip was over when they pulled into the ferry terminal. Zed soon discovered how much he'd oversimplified things. He spent part of day four waiting for their ferry to arrive and keeping three antsy children entertained, finding it more challenging than he'd imagined. Finally, they drove onboard with a plethora of other passengers on their way north. Most were on vacation. Zed was making a life change. The crowd was excited, he was grumpy. He hoped this little adventure was not a foretelling of days to come.

Zed experienced a moment of uncharacteristic panic as he drove onto the boat's car deck. He didn't have any issues with the boat itself; after all, he was a member of the U.S. Navy. It was the finality of the act of boarding. This was a place of no return. Was he ready to take on all he'd started with the Navy, his family and Alli? He contemplated those questions as he watched the ferry crew cast off, and the ship pull away from the port.

Zed looked at his tired children, having spent half the day running on every available green space in the area surrounding the ferry port, screaming, exploring, just being kids. He thought of the training center and the potential he had for continuing to give something valuable to the country he loved by training those who served the greater good. Teaching others how to protect their fellow man in all kinds of situations on domestic soil was a work he would be proud to be associated with. The success or failure of everything would be up to him, his expertise, and those he chose to accomplish the task. He hoped he'd chosen well.

He finally herded his little family back out of the car along with their personal go bags he'd taught them how to assemble. Tramping up the stairs to the purser, they grabbed their key and settled in for another two days, only this part of the journey was on a ferry. They'd seen plenty of ships. After all, their father was a naval officer, but to ride out into international waters, that was new. He put them into a four-berth stateroom, bribing them with snacks and technology while surviving every movie the boat showed on nearly a continual basis. He and the kids were desperate to arrive in their new island home or at least stop traveling.

The first days in the car were an adventure for everyone, but now they were ready for the novelty of setting up house on an island, in a community he expected them to grow up in. But now it was the last day of the trip, and he no longer shouted energetically for his children to see the wildlife, or spun tales of the Indians, the gold mines or the Oregon Trail. He didn't gather his offspring to see jumping fish or schools of seals, dolphins, whales. The bears on the beach were allowed to continue foraging, and the eagles overhead soared past with not more than a glance of interest. Zayden Wellesley, experienced Navy SEAL commander, prayed for land. He prayed for the same roof over his head for more than one day, and what kind of SEAL did that make him? A weary one.

His Chrissy would have loved it all. She would have calmed the grumpy cubs that found their way into the family SUV, but his skill set was different. Zayden was able to enjoy the ocean and the scenery when the children played with electronics or found other entertainment, and they seemed to get a kick out of the sunroom on the top deck. He kind of liked it too, but his fear for their safety had risen since their mother passed away, impeding some of his relaxed enjoyment.

Imaginings of unreasonable scenarios frayed his nerves as he watched his adventuresome children court the dangers of falling from the deck. The rail was high, his gut told him to settle the fuck down, but he was tired and obviously losing his grip if his kids were stressing him out on board ship. They seemed secure in the belief their father was invincible and would save them from all manner of disaster. They were right, he could have, but it still didn't lower his level of alertness.

Not for the first time, he acknowledged to himself that he was a much better SEAL on a mission than a parent at home. He never questioned his decisions on the job, but at home, parenting, it was all a crapshoot. Zed had spent long hours on transports over the ocean, always preparing for a mission or training of some kind. He'd not gotten his parenting sea legs. Now he would train others in preparation for homeland disasters and covert rescues, which was more in line with his current primary mission of keeping his own homefront free of disaster.

Zed missed a spouse's companionship, and until a few weeks ago, he'd missed sex. He wasn't a prude nor celibate, and his marriage hadn't been sedate, but he did like control, and his Chrissy was too shy to try new things. He'd happily covered his more dominant traits with her. She tended to rule the house because he was gone often. He led his team, she led the children. When he returned home, Chrissy tried to relinquish the reins and, for the most part, was successful, but it was hard for both of them.

Zed didn't know what was going on in the day-to-day operations at home and often didn't stay long enough to get established in those routines. He'd have been content to continue on that road for another four or five years, however, life changed.

Chrissy had been a perfect SEAL spouse, but now he needed different qualities. And he needed someone who loved his kids and him. He had to hope that would be Alli.

Zed spotted land and envisioned Alli standing on it. They'd survived, reaching Cache Island, alive and relatively unscathed. There were two small communities on Cache Island, Eagle's Landing and their destination, the town of Port Refuge. Mission accomplished. Zed appreciated the sunny sky now as he had on his recon trip, knowing it wouldn't last.

Rain was a common sight in this part of the world, snowstorms, high winds reaching gale force, and sunshine all in lesser quantities but still common during certain times of the year. Muskeg, waterfalls, dense forests, islands revealed only in low tide, mountain ranges, salt and freshwater sources all added to the magnificence of the area. Perfect for their rough terrain maneuvers and training — and curious children.

Life would slow down now for everyone. He'd be home most nights. Whether that was profitable to any of their sanities, remained to be seen. He would go occasionally, but those times would be few and far between instead of the other way around. His job now was stationary. He'd been gone for greater than half their little lifetimes, and the children deserved more of him.

Maybe he'd get a boat. These were incredible waterways. Spreading their wings, flying in different skies, and swimming different waters was exciting in its own way. Well, it would be once he got some decent shuteye and a familiar routine under their belt.

"Okay, kids, let's go get Uncle Chopper."

"Yay!" came three ecstatic responses.

"Is Uncle Chopper going to stay with us?" asked Kade.

"Visit for now. We will see about later, okay, buddy?"

"Okay."

Darrell "Chopper" Frazier, like Ryder Mason, was from Zayden's first SEAL team, and later, Zed's C.O. recruited Chopper. Chopper landed in DEVGRU right behind Zayden. Zed met Chrissy within two years of joining DEVGRU. Knowing he needed rank for decent pay, he landed a leadership position that shortened his promotion time. A year later, he and Chrissy married, and a year after that, she was pregnant with Katrina. Knowing his job painted a target on his back, he traded his coveted spot to join a team locally but quickly shifted when the team leader spot came open on the west coast, near family.

Chopper, who had done a four-year stint with the Delta's, soon followed. Ryder took a different route, deciding paperwork and being on the strategic side suited him better after eight hard years on the ground. That's where they met River Bennett. He had made a similar career shift with Ryder in strategic command. Chopper, Zed and their team owed many saves to Ryder and River. If River, being from this part of the world, ever left the ground, Zed would snatch him up in a heartbeat.

Chopper piloted all types of transport. The man could pilot or fix anything in the air and most things on land and sea. Whenever the team needed a lift, in flew Chopper. He had an uncanny ability to know when to swoop in. He'd saved Ryker and Zed's bacon more times than was natural.

On his way north to explore another job potential, Chopper agreed to check out the base here for possible acceptance of a position. His former team had lost two and retired two. With the changes going on, and his body telling him to look at alternative games to play, he was considering Zed's offer.

After giving the children an hour to rest, they headed over to the café to get the news of the community, good coffee, and to feed Chopper and the kids. Zed called Jennifer and told her he was back in town and would drop by shortly. He knew as soon as she realized he had children Alli would know.

He sent Chopper and the kids on ahead. Chopper was always hungry, and today the children were as well. All Zed could think about was his disclosure. He thought he'd take a run over to the new house and check on it in hopes of also seeing Alli. It would allow him to break the news that he was a father of three, before presenting them.

It continued to bother him ever since he knew the feelings he had were more than lust. He'd essentially lied about a huge part of his life. It was common for Zed to be secretive about all areas of his life, but this went beyond that. Alli had said she would be out of town, and she was. He had asked for honesty and acted as though the same rules didn't apply to him. Damn. Well, he'd check on the house and the workers before they knocked off for the day and then he'd head back to the café.

"Hey, there's the new family mom called me about," Jennifer told her friend over the phone. "Now, you know I'm no gossip, but word is he didn't bring a wife with him. After I go back home in the fall, guess who is coming back and needs perking up?" Alli knew she was referring to their college roommate.

"She doesn't need a man to do that. Not now and probably not for a long time."

"*Pfft*. Casey could use a diversion that didn't require a commitment. I hear SEALs are all about that."

"Not all of them," chided Alli. "Anyway, you said family so the man must have kids. Sounds like all kinds of commitment."

"He does, three of them, but he had to do something to make them, didn't he? I tell you, reading books is a far cry from the real thing. How did we rate two Navy SEALs?"

"Maybe this one came because of Zed," said Alli.

"This one is another demi-god, like your Zayden only golden. Too bad you don't have your cell. I'd send you a picture. He's tanned with incredible blue eyes and blonde hair. Nearly as tall as your Zed. And he has some heavy-duty muscles if that stretched tee shirt is any indication."

"I miss Zayden. He'll get back any day, and I'll be back in a couple of days."

"Oh, didn't I tell you? Zed called and said he'd be in later to pick up his lunch. He got back in town today and is looking for you. I told him you weren't home yet. He sure missed you by the sound of his disappointment."

"Good because I missed him, too. Hey, I need to turn the satellite phone off. See ya in a couple days."

Now that she knew he was in town, Alli wished she could magically whisk home. She tried to remind herself that patience was a virtue but ended up reminding herself of all the luscious ways that man had fired her rockets. It was soon all she could think of, and the wait became an albatross. She'd spent every quiet moment thinking of him and some not so quiet moments. Alli was hooked on that man, and while she would never admit it, she hoped she'd hooked him too.

She saw something in Zayden that she'd not seen in Chad: respect. He saw her as an equal. It was true he had antiquated ideas, but he didn't push them on her. He'd allowed her to accept or decline. Not that he didn't try to persuade her, something he was rather good at, but still, he allowed her to make her own decisions. Being with him, she felt safe, sheltered. Priceless.

What would it be like to share a life with a man like Commander Wellesley? Have and raise children with him? Learn more about him and who he was deep inside. She always had lots of fun at culture camp with the children, but now, knowing Zayden was in town and moving into the house next to her, she couldn't wait to get home and see him again, maybe even make plans with him.

She'd be home soon enough, and the future would begin.

Chapter Eight

Zed entered the café just as his gang was finishing their meal. "Hey, Jenn." He kissed her cheek. "Got my lunch packed up?"

"Yep. Let me get it."

"Hey, when is Alli back?"

"Saturday afternoon."

"Okay, thanks. Don't tell her I'm here, will you? I want to surprise her."

"Um, yeah, about that..."

"You already told her. How?"

"She called me on the camp's satellite phone to see if you got in yet." Jenn cringed as she continued. "I might have said you called. Sorry. But really, it's for the best. You know she isn't much for surprises, right?"

"Yep. We're working on that."

"Good luck."

"I see you took care of Chopper and the kids. Thanks."

"Oh, yeah. He's a hunk, and the kids are well-mannered. Let me get your lunch."

When she came back out, Zed was paying at the register, and the blonde man he'd called Chopper was heading out the door, kids in tow. Zed snagged the bag, waved, and left. Later that evening, he took the children to get root beer floats at the library, at the cashier's suggestion. After returning to the B&B he'd booked, and settling the children in bed, he relaxed with a glass of wine. Zed had dropped off Chopper so he could check out the nightlife. Zed wondered how active it was.

After chatting about local events during the summer, he discussed the plans he had for the new house. Jacqui Williams, Jennifer's mother, and owner of the B&B approved of Zayden's house choice.

"You'll love living next to Alesha."

"I think we will too. Alli showed me the town last time I was here. I enjoyed her company and know the kids will enjoy living there."

"She's always busy, that girl, but I think part of that is because she's lonely. Jenn says Alli wants to settle down but is afraid to head in that direction, thanks to that guy she dated for four years."

"I heard a little about him."

Zed didn't want to talk about Alli's private life to others. It wasn't his place to do that, and having lived keeping military secrets for the last fourteen years, it didn't sit well sharing about another's life without them there or without their permission.

Jacqui continued. "When she's ready, I'm sure she'll tell you more. And that worthless Craig Harlow has been bothering Alli. It is more of harassment now. He won't quit calling her and telling her she owes him for the way she left the last date. She puts up a good front, but I overheard him last week. The things he says to her are crude, and if I were her, I'd file a complaint. Alli refuses, saying there isn't anything she can do. She doesn't want to make it worse, so she leaves it."

"What did he say, exactly?" Zed's voice was quiet, and his tone appeared calm. He was anything but relaxed. His training allowed him to control his reactions while still plotting how he would get rid of Craig. Not the way he wanted to get rid of him, but in a sanctioned or at least nontraceable way.

"You know, calling her names in the four-letter category. It horrified me and, I'm worried about how far that man will go. You know, he had her backed against a building down one of the side roads and if it wasn't for a trooper friend just driving by, no telling what would have happened. He got a warning on that one."

"That needs to stop," said Zed harshly.

"Yes, it does."

Jacqui and Earl, her husband, both yawned, and Zed found he wanted to encourage them going to bed so he could play some night games. He'd get Chopper to come play with him. It would be a fast in and out, but it would be enough.

"Guess we all need some shut-eye," said Zed.

"It's been a long day, for sure. Good night, Zed."

"Goodnight."

Zed had made a fool of Harlow when he'd saved Alli from his lecherous clutches, and now he was making her life miserable. He should have been more clear he had claimed Alli that night, so there was no misunderstanding she was his. Zed had well and truly claimed her at that moment. No, Craig Harlow needed to be taught a lesson.

He must have thought Zed was gone and not coming back so he could do what he wanted. It was the only explanation because the man surely wasn't that stupid as to mess with a SEAL's woman. Time to disabuse the man of that erroneous thinking. He opened his encryption program and pulled up Craig's address. The idiot allowed his home address to be brandished across the internet as though it were a badge of honor. Zed sent an encrypted message to Chopper.

"Playground."

Zed had allowed the kids to play for an hour at the little playground they passed a few blocks from Chopper's hotel. He knew, no matter where Chopper was, he'd drop everything and show up. Zed checked the children and satisfied they were sound asleep, he slipped out the door and headed for the rendezvous.

Zed was glad he'd brought his voice changer. It would take Harlow a while to find a way out of the zip ties, though. They'd blindfolded him and had tape over his mouth. It would surprise Zed if the man even knew there were two of them. The whole scare routine was over in a few minutes. It took longer to dispose of the latex gloves and the plastic ponchos. Finding six different garbage cans isn't as easy as it sounds in a small community.

"Damn, Wellesley, you took a whole hour. I told my piece of sugar I'd be back already."

"I sincerely hope you are finding legal entertainment?"

Chopper looked offended. "I don't pay. I offer, they accept."

Zed shook his head. "You'll find another if that one is gone."

"True that."

"You need to find a girlfriend."

"I'm always looking, just haven't found one yet."

"Zero nine hundred, The Wharf. The café doesn't open 'til ten."

"Roger that."

By the time Zed crawled into bed, it was almost midnight. The deed was done. They caught Craig just as he was going into his house. Zed made quick work of explaining the way a gentleman behaved without giving themselves away or laying a harming finger on him or the loss of even one drop of blood.

This was not the first time they had put a little fear in a waste of space like Harlow. His CO, some years ago, had a daughter who was being harassed. They had executed a scare, and the kid decided he wasn't as interested in messing with innocent young girls anymore. He hoped Harlow came to the same conclusion.

It took a while for Zed to stop his brain from thinking about Alli and the things he needed to accomplish before his leave was up. The contractor said he'd finish tomorrow. Zed hoped he was right because transitions were hard, and he wanted to be in the house when Alli came home. He might still have a chance to head off disaster if he could get to her before the kids.

Zayden lay in bed and thought of Alli's smooth skin, flushed with the heat of arousal. How her nipples hardened into deep red raspberries as he loved her. He could hear her little mews and squeaks when she wiggled under his teasing fingers. His cock, even as his mind pulled out the memories, grew hard and uncomfortable. He missed her even more now that he was this close to her than when he was several thousand miles away. Here, it was as though his body told him he didn't need to deny himself. He hoped that remained true after he confessed.

The next morning Zed first stopped to let Chopper and the kids out to see the house, but since there was still debris everywhere, he didn't allow the children more than an outside look. Chopper took a quick tour before climbing aboard the transport with the gang, headed to the base. Zed showed them around the training center and building as he got an update on the work. The place looked incredible, and the contractor had already incorporated the suggestions he'd made. This would more than meet their needs. There was room to grow this program to an impressive size. It might include two teams.

"Look, a helipad just for you. I wanted a place we could get in and out of quickly, both for real-life and simulation. There are several helipads on Cache, and the circle is paved in front of the house, so you'd be able to land on the mainland and jump the boat or vice versa with little effort."

"I see what you're doing here. It doesn't have to be me. You'd do well with anyone who flew on your team."

"They would do, but they wouldn't be the best. You're the best."

Chopper grinned. He was the best, and there was no denying it. Just as he opened his mouth to tease his friend, another officer showed up.

"Commander Wellesley?" Zed reached out his hand, and the officer shook it. "Mark Chambers. I got a call you were on your way. Glad you got here okay. I assume you're on leave and setting things up for your family."

"Affirmative. This is Lt. Colonel Darrell Frazier, Marine Corps. I forgive him for his branch because he's been Navy, Army, and now the Marines. He's saved my ass enough times to make up for it," laughed Zed. "I'm trying to recruit this old man as my team pilot." The men laughed and swapped war stories as the children explored. "I hear you're previous Special Forces yourself, Colonel. Too bad you've your own command, I could have used a man like you on the ground maneuvers."

Mark laughed. "In my younger days, I was hell on wheels, but now I'm content to head operations on the research and testing site here. We'll be working together even though what we do won't crossover. With me leading one end and you leading the other, it should be a wild ride. I've heard about you from a couple of my buddies."

"And I've had a look at your history. First name's Zayden. Most call me Zed."

"I appreciate it, Zed. Call me Mark."

When there was a lull in the conversation, Chopper looked around. "Accommodations are decent, the company good. I might be back before you know it, gentlemen."

Zed took a deep breath and relaxed further. "Anytime, Chopper. You know, over the years, I haven't spent many vacations with the family, and I'm looking forward to this new lifestyle."

"I know that bittersweet feeling when I put a stop to midnight airdrops and early morning swamp runs," said Chambers. The men drifted back to personal memories. Colonel Chambers spoke into the silence. "I think you'll enjoy living here. The kids will; guaranteed. The Fourth of July is a big thing around here, too. They have a carnival of sorts, a festival, parade and community events. They are rather good at celebrating all the holidays. Look up the community calendar, and don't forget to subscribe online to the newspaper. You'll get everything that's news fast that way.

"I'm going on leave next week and won't be back till the fifth. If you need anything, call the office. I'll leave them your phone number. If there's a question from any of your guys, my office will forward them to your cell phone."

"Sounds like a plan, Mark. See you in a few weeks." Zed's small group left for the boat and lunch.

As Jenn treated the children to macaroni and cheese with hot dogs, against Zed's expressed instructions, Chopper and Zed spoke to several of the local fire and rescue people having lunch at the same time. They discussed the opportunities the training center could offer them as local civil servants. Zed also asked for suggestions on what they wanted in the way of training.

Search and rescue was the extent of what they did on the island. There was no need for things like kidnap extractions in hostile environments like other states had. There had been a hostage situation involving some transplant from down south, but otherwise, it was straightforward. The group invited the two men to a breakfast meeting on Saturday with the community groups that included bush medical personnel. Chopper would stay for that before flying his plane north to check out his original opportunity.

Zed returned to the table and the kid's lunch. He looked at Jenn, his words delivered in a voice deep and chastising. "Jennifer, I told you good food."

She shrugged. "They think it tastes good. You two shouldn't have left me to babysit. And that voice you just pulled, Zayden Wellesley? Save it for Alli and your minions. I don't intimidate easily."

Zed and Chopper burst out laughing. Zed said, "I stand corrected, maybe you are where Alli gets it from."

"Gets what?"

"Her obstinate tendencies."

"I could help you with that problem," offered Chopper.

"Sorry, golden god, I have a boyfriend."

Chopper shrugged. "If you ever change your mind, I'm game."

Jenn shook her head and went to the kitchen. Zed wondered if she would betray his secret before he had a chance to disclose. He followed her into the kitchen to have a word. As they were finishing lunch, Zayden got a call. Still, no word from Alli, and he'd hoped it was her calling. Looking at the number, it was familiar but not recall familiar, so he knew it wasn't her. His disappointment hit him so hard that he almost missed answering the call.

"Wellesley."

"This Zayden?"

"It is."

"Hey, this is Trevor Dickson, your contractor. The house is ready for occupancy."

"That's great news. Thanks for the call. Can I meet you later this afternoon for the walkthrough? Two this afternoon would be great. Thanks again."

"Kids, the house is ready to move into." The kids whooped and hollered. "Let's go check it out."

"Hey, mind if I take a raincheck? Got things I need to check on myself."

"Care to share?"

"Not in mixed company. Hey, I'll see you in the a.m."

"Got it."

Zed looked over at Alli's house as they arrived at the little cul-de-sac. Alli's place was still dark. Zed did the walkthrough, went back over the contract details, and signed off on the house.

"We move in tomorrow, gang. Oh-seven-hundred." It sounded like a crowd cheering instead of three munchkins.

Later at the B&B, Zed prepared to load the SUV with their gear to be ready for the morning maneuvers. They would eat a quick dinner he would cook in the kitchen at the Williams' and then early bed. The hold baggage was to be delivered tomorrow afternoon. Friday. Alli should be home Saturday. He was as excited as a teenager with his first girlfriend, and at the same time, he dreaded the disclosure he would need to make and the accompanying fallout.

"I hope you have everything you need to settle in, dear," said Mrs. Williams.

Zed suppressed a smile. Only his mother dared call him dear, especially after he'd become a "trained military fighting machine," and looked the part.

"They will deliver our essentials tomorrow and the remainder when it hits the island." He paused. "Honestly, I wouldn't mind finding a good housekeeper or several good babysitters for when I go back to work," said Zayden.

"I'll ask around for sitters, but you won't find a housekeeper in the traditional sense. I know a few people that might come in a couple days a week. As for sitters, you could ask Alli. She's home during the summer."

Zed wasn't even sure that Alesha would speak to him after she found out he had three little replicas of himself, so he didn't answer other than to thank Jacqui for her suggestion and continue to pack. He was eager to move in, and if it weren't for the fact that the children were asleep in beds they wouldn't have tomorrow night in the house, he would have packed them up and taken them over now.

The next morning, after spending a restless night worrying about Alesha's reception and his dick demanding to feel her wrapped around it soon, he turned the kids loose on the house. He'd scored dad points when they began giggling and racing to see every nook and cranny. Zed had made them remain subdued while the work was underway and during the final inspection, preferring them to play outside, but today was freedom. He would call Chopper when the hold baggage showed up so they could assemble the beds.

"Daddy, someone gave us brownies!" squealed an excited five-year-old Kami. That brought not only her two siblings to the kitchen but a concerned father.

"Kami don't touch them," barked Zed.

"Aww," whined her twin, Kaden.

The cellophane-wrapped plate was one he recognized from Alli's place. Where was she? Her car had been gone since they arrived. He called her cell, but it went straight to voicemail. She wasn't even home yet, or was she? Now, it concerned him. He tried calling her again, and his call went straight to voicemail again. Katrina, his nine-year-old going on thirty, handed him an envelope with what he could only assume was Alli's handwriting. He hadn't seen it before.

Zayden,

Sorry that I wasn't there to meet you, but I did try to call. Anyway, I'm at culture camp this week. I thought brownies might appease you until I got back. I've missed you and hope your trip was uneventful. Here is my key if you need something there. See you soon.

Love, Alli

"Who is Alli, dad?"

"She's a friend and the lady who lives in the house next to us."

He'd grill for dinner tomorrow, keeping things festive and yet, low-key, helping Alli become comfortable with the children. He'd picked up a grill yesterday and left it in the garage. That is if he could clean up the dust and leftover debris the contractor had left behind. The majority of the house, besides getting a new garage door and some repairs such as the office flooring, didn't need any work. He'd had them gut the kitchen, which took an extra two weeks as they had to wait for materials the contractor ordered. Barges were not fast. The house would need general cleaning.

Kami yanked his tee-shirt.

"Daddy, can we eat the brownies now? They have that gooey candy in it."

Katrina filled in the blank. "Caramel, Kami, caramel." Katrina turned to face her father. "They do look good." Her eyes shined hopefully.

Zed, never one to miss the opportunity to use good incentives, said to the trio, "If you get your rooms swept out so they can deliver your things, I will allow you each one before lunch."

Kade, who loved a good challenge, yelled, "I'll be the first to get a brownie!" He took off toward his room only to return with a puzzled look on his face, "Daddy, we don't need to sweep, it's clean."

"Can't be, Kade, they worked in here. It's got to be dusty."

Zed checked, and sure enough, the floors and windows were clean, and now that he noticed, the dust was gone from every room not worked on. Alli. He loved her even more than he had when he boarded the plane weeks ago. And he wanted to roast her little behind for not doing as he'd told her and stay away. She had risked all that dust getting into her lungs.

He hadn't been able to get that woman out of his mind even though he had thought in the beginning it might have been just a little 'back in the saddle' event for both of them. It wasn't. Not for him. These acts of love, even in the face of disobeying orders, proved it wasn't for her either. Zed felt energized. The children took their brownies outside while he checked for what was next on his long to-do list just as the delivery truck arrived.

Chapter Nine

The next morning Zed was congratulating himself on breakfast. It had been a great idea. After spending time with these men and women, he was confident that accepting the training center and coming here was the best move of his career other than becoming a SEAL. He would still work with the same level of abilities, but the worry of leaving his children alone, possibly completely alone, with no parents, was off his shoulders. Of course, life happened, but it was more predictable now, less likely to be due to his career choices or radical terrorists.

After seeing Chopper off for parts north, Zed walked into his house with renewed satisfaction only to find it empty of little people. Because of the things he experienced in his adult life thus far, his mind was concerned, but his gut didn't quiver. Why weren't they home? He remembered a conversation with his mom when trying to decide on taking the assignment.

"No crime," everyone said.

"I see that, but it's because there isn't any population, mom."

"No," his mother said, "because everyone knows everyone, that's why. And because it has to be next to impossible to get off the island fast enough. They always get caught."

Zayden laughed. "Mom, how do you know all of this?"

"I researched the area and the little town on my own. It sounds wonderful. I'm going to love coming and visiting."

It felt good to have his own home, but if something had already happened to the kids, he would hate himself forever. He heard a noise in the other room. His shoulders relaxed, but his alert was still on high. Calling out, his sitter, a down-to-earth college student he'd been able to hire on his visit, walked out of the den.

"Hello, Mr. Wellesley." No disaster then.

"Hey, Samantha. I'm back and call me Zed."

"Okay, Zed. The kids are outside playing over at Miss Campbell's house."

"She's gone until this afternoon."

Samantha grabbed her pack, and the money Zed held out then pointed to the neighboring yard. "Guess she's back. See you later."

Damn, damn, damn. Why had he not told Alesha about the children? Zed stared across the yard at his offspring, his walking, talking, and now visiting bundles of joy, children were chatty Alesha's ear off. Zed prayed things would be all right. He was in so much hot water. He could see Alli was animatedly talking to them from here. Zed knew he should wait for the children's intel before rushing over there, but he needed to know what the children had told her so he could address the issue correctly. At least that was his story.

ALLI SMILED AT THE young chatterboxes in front of her. "Now help me out. This time the oldest goes first."

"I'm Katrina. I'm nearly ten, well in three months. Daddy said that they let me in school early because I'm smart, but I heard it's because I started school on base."

"I see. That makes you headed for the fourth grade. Impressive."

Katrina grinned proudly. "Yes, you get it."

"My turn now, Kat. Hi," said the young man as he put out his hand solemnly to shake Alli's. "I'm Kaden, but people call me Kade. And I'm five. I was born before Kami, so she's the baby. We go to kindergarten next year."

"Well, very nice to meet you, Kade. I think kindergarten is the most fun." That information brought a grin to the young gentleman.

"Me, it's me now. I'm Kami, well, Kameron." said the little girl in high ponytails that bounced with every word. "I'm the twin. And I'm not the baby, Kade. Daddy says I'm the youngest."

"I see. Well, I'm happy to have met you all. Now, where did you say you lived?"

"Right there." The children pointed to Zed's house, and Alli nodded.

"So, where is your father?"

"Oh," answered Katrina, sagely, "I think he's home now. Should I go find him? He doesn't have friends that are girls unless they are military. Not on his team but his friends. I think he needs to meet you. We shouldn't talk to people he hasn't met yet."

The twins were playing with a pile of stones, building something only they could see in their mind's eye. Alli and Katrina sat on the front steps of Alli's house. Katrina assumed a conspirator's look as she imparted her secrets to her newest friend.

"Alli," she started with a serious face, "I think you need to know some things about my daddy."

"Oh? Well, maybe he will tell me himself."

Katrina shook her head. "Don't count on it. You don't have to tell him I told you or anything, but if you know, you won't be surprised."

"Well, then maybe you had better tell me."

"Okay. Our mom died when I was six, and the twins were two. That was a long time ago. The twins don't even remember her. Sometimes I have trouble too. Daddy says we miss mommy, but we don't need another one. Me and grandma think he's wrong. Anyway, he's a nice Navy guy, a SEAL and everything. He looks okay, you know, for a dad, and the girls watch him like they like him, you know, the grownup ones. But he has a problem."

"Really?"

Did all the men in Zayden's life lose wives? Alli wondered if the children's mother was truly dead or did her father do as some parents did and simply say that so the children wouldn't think one parent abandoned them. Zed said it was not for everyone, being the spouse of a military member.

"Yes. Grandma says he has kids, and lots of mommies want to have their own children, you know? My grandma's smart, but she doesn't know this," Katrina leaned down in a conspirator manner. "I think Daddy is awfully bossy."

"Why would you say that?"

"I think he's bossy because," Katrina leaned in and whispered, "I think mommy didn't follow orders or something. He spanked her, and it made mommy laugh and make squealing noises."

"I see. Maybe they were playing around."

"Maybe it tickled, sometimes her eyes were red like she was crying. She said she had allergies, but..." said Katrina with obvious suspicion. Alli could see that wasn't something Katrina had thought of, nor was she inclined to believe. The little girl continued. "Maybe ladies don't like that game, you know like I hate tickling. He should probably stop if he wants a wife. I just don't want you to get mad if he plays like that with you because I think you're going to be perfect."

"Perfect?"

"To be our mommy. Of course, daddy will have to interview you, like he does everyone, but if you smile pretty, maybe he will decide to marry you. Oh, and don't tell him 'no.' Navy SEALs and daddies don't like to be told no."

"Really?"

Katrina shrugged. "Sure, everyone knows that."

"Well, sweetheart, I wouldn't worry. We're just neighbors, and it's just friendship."

"Too bad cause he likes you. But he might be mad at you right now."

"What? Why do you think that?"

"Because he was calling you, and you didn't answer him. And something about disobeying his direct order. But don't worry too much, I think he likes you, and if you like him, then he might not be mad anymore. Remember, he likes people to mind him. And smile a lot. He likes people who smile. Anyway, I thought I should warn you, but don't tell daddy. I don't think he knows that I know."

"About being upset?" Alli was feeling a little like Alice tumbling down the rabbit hole.

Katrina rolled her eyes. "No, that he spanks mommies when he plays."

Alli grinned and then hurriedly wiped it from her face. "Got it. Now you better get home before he finds you're cavorting with the enemy."

"Huh?" Katrina shook her head. "You're silly, you aren't the enemy. I told you, daddy likes you, but you have to stay out of trouble. My daddy *exnialates* the enemy. He doesn't want to do that to you."

"Annihilates?" Katrina nodded. "How do you know?"

"He said so. And he told Chopper he doesn't know why he had to fall for the stubborn one." Kat raced from the yard with a parting admonition. "Now, don't forget... bye."

It appeared the confidences were over as Katrina looked toward her siblings teasing and yelling to them, announcing she would beat them home. Kat followed Alli's directional stare and smiled. "I have to get these two a snack. Come on, let's get some junk food."

"Daddy said no more today," said Kami.

"Shh, it will be our secret. If you don't want it Kami, you can stay here, but Kade and I are hitting the cookie stash."

"I'm coming too."

The little group took off, running and waving as they disappeared in Zayden's house.

The children were adorable, but what about that father of theirs? And why were they at Zed's place? Jenn had told her when they had come into the Coffee Cache that their father was a blonde god. Was Zed letting his friend stay with him until they found a place? But according to Katrina, her father liked her. How could he? They hadn't met. Had Jennifer shown him a picture? She wouldn't do that.

Was Kat's father looking for a wife? Katrina said not, but who knew? What Kat had said about a mother was probably true. They needed a mother because they were too young to grow up without one, if at all possible. And to listen to the too observant little girl, Zed's friend shared similar bedroom habits. Must be it was a SEAL thing.

Alli thought of Zayden and their attraction. Was she mother material? She'd always thought she would get married and have children of her own. She'd been having dreams of children with Zayden. What would they look like? Dark headed with milk chocolate eyes, a bit of tan. Similar to the kids she'd just met. Their mother must have had dark features.

Alli met Samantha as a student-teacher when Alli helped the school do medical screenings. Samantha slowed down as she drove away from Zed's house next door. Alli smiled and waved. The young woman stopped and waited for Alli to walk up to the car.

"Have you met your new neighbor? That Zed Wellesley is some kinda hot."

Alli laughed. "Yes, I did last month. I agree he is good looking." Alli hoped she would not need to fend off all the college kids. Zed didn't seem like the kind to cradle snatch, but that wouldn't stop the young women from looking and hoping.

"Good thing too. With three kids and no wife, he will need all he can get in the sex appeal department."

Stunned, Alli verified what it sounded like Samantha said. "I thought those kids were Chopper's. You know, tall, nice looking blonde Navy guy."

"Nope never met him, but I promise you that those kids are Zed's. He just paid me for watching them, and he is the one who interviewed me last month. I have no doubt he is Navy. Haircut. Plus, he has that way about him. You know he's the one in control, and he doesn't have to say anything. That makes it even yummier. Gotta go." The car window went up, and Samantha waved as she drove away.

Katrina had been talking about Zayden all along. He thought she was stubborn, huh? *She* was the one Zed said he liked. None of that mattered right now because he'd lied to her. Lied by omission, if nothing else. She was steaming mad. Then she remembered his firm muscles and gentle touch. His commanding ways that sent the now-familiar hot flush ride along her skin. She'd wanted him incessantly since he left. It devastated her to think she was the only one who had those romantic feelings and pissed off that she still had them. There had to be an explanation. Right?

Her heart searched for the good. He sent her the plant and texted her. He really was a nice guy who had no trouble taking charge when necessary. Zed had been caring and protective even when he wasn't with her. He'd saved her from Craig. This man was special; she felt it deep down. Allie chided herself. What was she doing? He was a scoundrel of the first order, and he lied to her without shame. How did she do it again? She fell for him, hard. Were all men this attractive untrustworthy?

There was a knock at her door, and she'd little doubt who it would be. Zed wasn't a man to let things lie. He would address them head-on like now. Except it was obvious, she didn't rate honesty. She wouldn't give him a chance to change her mind. She could be just as formidable and commanding when it was important. Alli schooled her features to answer the non-verbal demand to let the man in. When she opened the door, her knees nearly buckled at the longing to be in his arms. Her irritation held her firm. Barely.

"Alli."

Chapter Ten

"**I** missed you, sweetheart."

There was affection and relief in his voice as he reached for her. Alli stepped back. He looked so good, she wanted to cry. His voice tugged her deeply, her core contracted, releasing liquid arousal. Her chest tightened in desire. She'd waited what seemed like forever to be in those arms, to feel that heat surround her. Her knees felt weak, and she wondered how long her legs would hold her up. Instead of reaching for him, she held firm, her voice cool.

"Zed. You made it."

His look was hesitant and hurt. Hurt? It was *her* prerogative to feel betrayed, given his lack of disclosure, not his.

"Yes, but you already know that." How dare his voice carry any censure in it! "Can I come in?"

Katrina's words sounded rude in her head. Yes, Katrina hit her father's mannerisms on the head, but he was so much more.

"Of course, you *can*, but I don't know if I want you to." Her tummy was pinging again at the sound of his deep, calm voice. She wanted him so damn bad. "I'm not sure what to think right now."

"Alesha." The pause was for effect, and it did its job. "Let me in, sweetheart. I'll explain everything."

That voice. You'd think Zed was talking to a naughty child. A naughty, *beloved* child that belonged to him. Her tummy tingled again, and her core danced a little jig. *Traitor*. Tears welled in her eyes, and she absolutely hated it.

He pleaded well in a controlling sort of way. Alli stepped back to allow Zed inside and closed the door behind him before she'd even processed what she'd done. Too late, she remembered she didn't want to hear his excuses. Yet, here he stood in her entryway, in expectation of what? The entryway was much smaller with him in it, and she fought the urge to step into his arms. He'd invaded her breathing space but didn't touch. She ached for his kiss. His thumbs wiped her tears, and she had to fight hard to stop them from taking over. Her mind fought her disloyal body. Turning without a word, she led him to the kitchen and offered him coffee, all with jerky movements of forcing her body to do what it didn't want to do, resist.

"No, thanks. I had my fill at breakfast this morning."

She nodded and poured herself another cup before sitting at the table. Zed walked to the stand that held the pot of flowering plants he'd sent.

"Needs water, don't you think?"

"Yes, I've been gone and forgot to tell someone to take care of it. I guess I'm not the only one that feels neglected. However, I did overwater it before I left." She took a deep breath praying she wouldn't break. "So, obviously, you aren't the only one who forgets things, except, in this case, I think my transgression is easily trumped by yours."

"Alesha."

"Why didn't you tell me?"

Zed sat at the table. "Everything I said was true about my wife, my career, those incredible days with you. I was going to tell you everything, but when you said you needed the quiet after a day working, I knew you wouldn't get that with me. I wanted you to know me, want me, maybe even love me a little before I sprung them on you. My hope was that maybe you would consider giving up the solitude if you connected to me enough." He bowed his head and reached for her hand. She pulled it out of his grasp. Touching him would be her undoing.

"But you didn't give me a chance to talk about it. You weren't honest with me. That's the foundation on which trust is formed."

"Alli, I feared it was too soon. Once we got here, I left the kids with my friend Chopper and went to tell you I was back and about the children, but you weren't here." She resented the sliver of accusation in his tone.

"Obligations, Zayden. Obligations that you were fully aware of and that I told you about before you came back. You didn't treat me with that same courtesy." She wanted to dump him, tell him to take his secrets and leave her alone, but she didn't have the strength. Just the sound of his voice, the sight of him sent her libido and her desperation to be held by him, into the red zone. She'd honestly never felt this way about someone. No one, not even after four years with Chad, had ever reached her on such a visceral level that she had no defenses. Instead, she went on the offensive.

"So, what were you going to do, act like we didn't do what we did, or have what we had? I thought it meant something to you. Obviously, I was wrong."

The words tumbled out as her heart raced in protest. Alli stood up, scraping her chair back, to walk further into the kitchen and lean against the sink. It allowed her a safe distance from him. He was too enticing. She yearned for him too much to be physically close right now.

"Time for complete disclosure."

"That would be refreshing, although I doubt it will make a difference now. You're familiar with the adage, 'too little too late,' I presume."

He frowned but didn't take the bait. Damn him. Alli was spoiling for a good shouting match.

"Alli, I didn't expect to fall for you. I was immediately attracted to you, and it took me by surprise. At first glance, I thought we might be a hook up while I was here but didn't imagine it could be more. There was no doubt you were out of my class. You're younger than I am, probably by some years."

"You're kidding, right? Every woman in town that has seen you has turned to watch you. Without much effort, you could have every single woman on the island and a few not so single."

"I doubt it, but even if it were true, I hadn't taken a woman, who wasn't my wife, on a date in a dozen years. The second year after Chrissy's accident, I hooked up with a couple of women, pick-ups after missions before coming stateside and nothing else. I'm not proud of it, and I soon learned it wasn't for me. I had no working knowledge of how things went these days. Foolish, I know, but I'd watched my young frogs as they wandered the ports and thought I'd need to emulate some of their behaviors. But honestly, they mostly picked up frog hogs, and I didn't care to partake."

"'Frog hogs?'"

Zed grimaced. "Women who only pick up who they believe to be SEALS, but Frogs are anyone who can work underwater combat tasks. The women don't intend to stay, just play. Once we spent that first afternoon together, I couldn't risk you slipping away without getting closer to you. I don't mind saying I worked double-time to get you interested. Instead of a simple hook up, I fell hard for you, and by then, the time for disclosure seemed to have passed."

"It was at that exact moment you should have told me you had three children."

"I was going to introduce you to them. I screwed up, I get it, but those children are my life. I wanted to bring you together with them but needed to tread carefully. A part of me worried you would love them and not me. Or love me but not be agreeable to raise another woman's children. I knew I should have said something when I left, but by then it was too late."

She shook her head but didn't speak as he continued.

"Alli, I was trying to protect myself and the children and woo you at the same time. I miscalculated and messed up." He laughed mirthlessly. "I don't usually do that. I'm a planner. I'm confident and understand the outcomes of all avenues of choice. When I make decisions in my professional life, I know the consequences. In my private life, I protect at all costs. That's what I was doing. But honey, I haven't been able to do anything but think of you since I first laid eyes on you. Please tell me this incredible short-sightedness on my part doesn't end what I know is good, could be extraordinary."

Alli looked at Zed, and her heart melted. It made sense even if she wished he'd trusted her enough to tell her about his children. He hadn't known her then. She imagined it would be hard to trust someone with even the knowledge of your children right away. Foolish even. She would have probably thought less of him if she was on the outside looking in and seen him fully accept someone he had only spent a few days getting to know. He couldn't have trusted that person enough to expose his young children to them. She knew what had to happen.

Alli shook her head. "I don't know if we can make this work, Zayden. Katrina told me to watch out and smile nicely at you."

"What?"

"She said you had a problem." Alli tried to stay as somber as she could.

"She did? I'm sure she's right. Which problem, exactly?"

"You're bossy, and you spank."

"What? How does she... I swear, I don't... I would *never* lay a finger on my children."

"Evidently, she must have overheard a few things and puzzled out that you spanked your wife, and she wanted to make sure I knew ahead of time. I don't think she knew in what capacity that spanking occurred, but she was worried I might not know that about you. She, at least, is into full disclosure. She said I would be a perfect person to be her mommy, but you would have to interview me, like everyone else. Oh, and you don't like to be told 'no.'"

"She is too old for her years. Decades too old. And correct on all counts."

Alli laughed. Zed grinned. "I suppose I'll need to talk to her, but damn if I know how."

"No, don't. Katrina will think I have betrayed her confidence. Besides, she might be embarrassed to talk to you about it. I'd let it go. Years from now, if she remembers, she'll figure it out."

"How did you get so smart?"

"I'm not. I've just had my listening skills honed, and I'm not Katrina's parent. I listen to what she said between the lines. Parents who already think they know all about their child, don't tend to that as much. And a nurse always knows more about what makes people tick."

"Well, not always smarter. I seem to remember telling a certain nurse to stay out of the house while the work was going on, and since it wasn't finished until we arrived, I know that she didn't mind me."

"Yes, about that, Katrina told me about that too."

"She did? What did she say exactly?" He ventured a kiss on the column of her neck, nuzzling close and inhaling her scent.

"Um, well," she couldn't think when he was that close. "Something about you being mad at me and that you said I 'disobeyed a direct order.'"

"You did."

"Well, I waited until they were gone for the evening."

"Even worse because there wouldn't have been anyone to help you if something happened."

"I'm sorry?" Her apology sounded snarky. She smiled.

"Uh, huh. Insubordinate and unrepentant. So when shall we set up your interview?"

"Oh." She smiled again and shrugged her shoulders. "I'll have to check my calendar."

"You do that, but if I don't get a proper kiss of forgiveness and apology, then I might have to spank you."

"Maybe we can negotiate." She winked audaciously as her insides jumped for joy.

"Looks like I'm going to need to soundproof the bedroom. I anticipate telling noises inside."

"What about consent?" She smiled as she tingled all over.

"Remind me to explain the concept of *implied consent*."

"Oh."

She watched as he stepped in front of her, drawing her close as he dipped his head. He was going to kiss her properly now, and she wanted it more than her next breath. His first attempt was delivered softly, too softly. Alli wanted more, needed more of this man. She made a sound of frustration as she opened her mouth in invitation. Zed immediately accepted the offer, slipping his tongue inside, moving into a more ardent advance, plundering and soothing before he broke the connection and stepped back.

Pulling her close again, he rested his chin on the top of her head and settled his breathing as his large hands rubbed her back.

"We good now?"

"Maybe."

He kissed the top of her head. "No maybes. Sorry, the kids are alone next door and as mature as Katrina is, twins are nothing to shake a stick at. Come to dinner? We're grilling."

"Um, do I get to meet this blonde demi-god Jenn is talking about?"

He chuckled. "I'm the only man you need to worry about, young lady. Chopper is a good friend, but he's on his way north.

You'll meet him eventually, but we can enjoy just the family tonight."

"Okay, but we're still talking about this. You aren't off the hook yet."

"Yes, ma'am. Communication is usually my forte." He grinned. "I've been told I can be pretty persuasive." He kissed her lips hard. "Come over whenever."

DINNER WAS DELICIOUS, and they all helped clean up. Zed had his children in an assembly line they appeared to be familiar with. "Daddy, where does Alli go for her chore?" asked Katrina.

"Miss Campbell is a guest, and guests don't help."

"She's not a guest, she's our neighbor," said Kaden. "And Kat said she's going to be—" Katrina's hand clamped hard over her brother's mouth.

"It doesn't matter what Katrina said, I'm the boss, remember?"

The children replied as all good military kids did, "Yes, sir."

"But daddy, she isn't Miss Campbell, she's Alli. She told us to call her Alli," said Kami.

"Okay," said Zed in defeat as he smiled into Alli's eyes, brimming with amusement. "Alli can put the dining room back in order."

"Is that a real job, daddy?" asked Kami skeptically.

"It is today. Besides, you know that if I say it is, then it is."

Alli took a dishcloth and returned to the dining room, but as she left the kitchen, she heard Katrina ask him, "Daddy, are you going to kiss her?"

Alli didn't hear his reply, but she sincerely hoped he did more than that.

AS THE FAMILY FINISHED putting away the final bits of their delivered hold baggage, Monday morning, the rest of the furniture showed up. He should have just put it all together because the two days in between deliveries hadn't helped him much. Hold baggage was for those things needed immediately to last in the new quarters while waiting for your larger furniture shipment. He imagined they might have arrived on the same barge but instructed on which to deliver first. Alli couldn't understand the stupidity of it all.

"This is so much better than a buddy of mine, whose furniture, when he was returning from an accompanied tour overseas, went to Alaska and Hawaii before finding him on the east coast."

Alli looked at him in amazement. "How could that even happen?"

"He was reassigned to Hawaii to a special unit there from the east coast three months after arrival, prompting the error of diverting his furniture to Hawaii. After nine months and still no furniture, he returned to the east coast."

"So how did it get to Alaska."

"He left Hawaii because he was at his re-enlistment date. Instead of getting out, he took the old assignment on the east coast again and didn't swear in until the day he left. That paperwork got lost in the PCS transit, so they thought he had left the military."

"Oh, you have got to be kidding me."

"Nope. His home of record was Alaska, and the furniture swung by there on its way east. Finally, after eighteen months, he had his furniture, right after his wife divorced him. Life sucks sometimes."

"Incredible."

Zayden was well aware he'd dodged the bullet with Alesha. There was less keeping her with him than his buddy and wife.

Alli and Katrina were coming behind him and rearranging things to their liking. Well, he had the study and the garage to call his own. Even in his bedroom, Zayden expected to be taken over at some point. He hoped it happened sooner rather than later and made sure to leave his possible roommate space.

Zed stepped out onto the driveway after he finished setting up the garage. It had been a find that this house had one. Many didn't. There was so much rain, he didn't know why they all didn't have one. When you considered they were built on the side of a mountain, it began to make sense. They had, over the years, extended the useable land by artificial means including blasting and taking that blasted rock to extend the stable ground into the inlets and passages. In all the vast beauty, the terrain was still rough, unforgiving, and any flat ground was in short supply.

The stillness was, at times, deafening, but if you listened well, you could hear all manner of life and environment: waterfalls, jumping fish, birds, rodents, and three chattering children. He looked around for his gang and was in time to see his little busybodies race across Alli's small lawn. She looked to have just returned from a run, something he hadn't done in over a week. He allowed himself the memory of the exhilaration of a long calming run. He'd get that back on track as soon

as possible. Zed could only imagine what his children were saying.

KAMI LOOKED AT ALLI as she stretched. "You run? My
daddy does too. You could run with him."

"Well, hello, Kami. I usually run by myself, and I bet your
daddy does too."

"No," said Kade, "He usually runs with his team."

"His team? What kind of team is he on?"

"You know, the guys," added Kami.

Katrina came out of the back yard after checking on the
flowers she'd helped to plant and filled in the blanks. "SEAL
team. My dad is a Navy SEAL, remember? Well, at least he was
until we moved here. I think he still is, he said he was just doing different SEAL work. You know, he's training them, and
lots of guys like them." Kat thought for a quick minute and
continued. "You know, kinda like you. He's a teacher to other
grownups only in Navy talk he's called an instructor. I told you
he needs to stay closer to us since we don't have a mom." She
gave Alli a severe look. "It's too hard to find a housekeeper or a
babysitter that stays. So, he needs a wife."

"Right, I remember," answered Alli, who tried hard not to
laugh. She wondered if Katrina would be a negotiator in her
adult life. The girl was persistent if nothing else.

For the millionth time, she thought about what it would be
like to be the wife of such a man. Her cluttered bedroom would
be a thing of the past. And she was sure that leaving her tools
in the garage wherever they landed would be a definite call for
a more disciplined life. Alli suppressed a giggle when she imag-

ined drills where she would have to time how long she took to return the equipment to its rightful place. And if she didn't do it well, he would reach into the equipment closet and–

"What do you think about keeping an eye on us this summer?"

"What do you mean?" She knew what the too mature nine-year-old was saying, but she wanted it spelled out.

"You know, watch us while daddy goes to work. He has to go sometime after the Fourth of July."

"I see. Well, who was going to watch you?"

"He wants someone he can trust, and he trusts you. I mean, he likes you, so he must trust you."

"Did he tell you that?"

"Well, no, my grandma did, but he did say he needed a sitter. So, will you?"

"Will I what?"

Kat sighed in her exasperation. "Be our sitter."

"What about Samantha."

"Oh, um, she doesn't like us. Too many kids."

"She seemed happy enough when I talked to her."

"People change their minds, you know."

"Well, your dad would have to ask me and only occasionally, not every day."

"Yippee! Kami, Kade, she said yes!"

Alli looked up and saw the subject of their conversation stalk across his yard towards them. He had an intense determined look about him. Alli was discovering he was probably the reason Kat was so serious. She couldn't help watching him walk on those powerful legs encased in form-fitting jeans. Determined wild animal on the prowl, came to mind. He was a dangerous man in many ways, and she suddenly had to stifle a laugh. These girls were never going to get a date while they lived at home. Just the sight of Zayden Wellesley on protection detail would send every prospective suitor packing. The effect on her sex was a gush that required a change of panties. In the field he would be formidable, in her bedroom, he was explosive.

"What did she say 'yes' to exactly, Katrina Wellesley?"

"She can watch us sometimes."

"You did not ask her something I specifically forbid you to do." It was a statement of fact. Erroneous but still a statement.

Katrina lowered her head. "Well, you don't get all the decisions."

"In our family, I do. March into your room and take your siblings with you."

"Into my room?"

Zed hesitated for a moment. "You're so literal sometimes. Go home. All of you. Double time. Do not return without expressed authorization."

He turned to follow them, but Alesha placed her hand on his to stop him.

"Zed, don't be too severe. I honestly was just talking to her. I'm sure it just tumbled out."

Zed's face was grim. "When you learn my daughter better, Alli, you'll find that she does not do anything by chance. Usually, she is obedient, but there are those days that I need to remind her who runs our home. She's easy. An hour in her room and then helping me clean bathrooms should just about do it. The stubborn one is Kami."

Alli laughed. "I thought your housekeeper Kerry cleaned bathrooms."

Zed grinned. "She does, and that is what will irritate Kat the most, wasting her time."

"She is so like her father."

Zayden stopped talking and let his heated stare do it for him. Alesha filled in the void as she looked away to speak. "Um, anyway, come back if you find the available help isn't enough. I can't offer more than a day or two during the week, and a couple of weeks this summer, I won't be available, but hopefully, that will help."

Zed ran his hand lightly over her skin, surprising her at his gentleness. The tingling was so intense, it could have sent her tummy into the nationals for acrobats. She dipped her head. His finger slid under her chin and raised it.

"I need quiet time with you. Alone. I haven't had to take so many cold showers in my life."

"So, don't. Come over when the kids go to sleep."

"Or, even better, come to my bed. I won't worry about the kids, and you can stay all night."

"Is it soundproofed yet?"

He smiled. "Working on it. It's harder post-build. Until then, you'll have to be quiet."

She nodded and grinned back. "We'll see."

"Roger that." He dropped another kiss. "Go shower, sweetheart."

EARLY THE FOLLOWING morning, Zed decided it was high time to resume his routine. Alli had slipped into his bed last night, but they'd both been so tired. He'd barely started loving her when she'd fallen asleep. Zed was fast behind her.

Rising at 0600 hours, he put on his gear and took off. It was amazingly difficult to leave Alli's warm, sleeping body in bed. He almost gave up the run to make love to her.

After he'd clocked thirty minutes out, he turned around to return home, his home. That felt good. Alli had handled the children's visits and antics well so far, and he held out hope that she was getting used to the idea of having them in her life because he was determined to have her in his.

How his children were up before the chickens in the summer and dead to the world on a school day, he'd yet to figure out, but here they were again, sitting with the woman that an hour earlier, he'd left warm in his bed.

"Are they bothering you?" He asked as he came to stand even with the small group, his voice raspy with his panting.

"Nope, I was just waiting for you so I could go for a run, and they stopped me before I could start. While I loved the distraction, I really need to get going before I lose what little motivation I have."

"I love to run. Where do you go?"

"Well, when it isn't pouring, like today, I run down to Wolf Pack Pier and back."

"Not if there are real wolves there."

She smiled. Yep, bossy, arrogant. Demanding. More now than their time before Zed's move, she could see his true character. It wasn't just his position in the military, the man simply liked to give orders. It still didn't bother her too much hearing him give them so long as he didn't think she would pay attention. She was more of a live and let live kinda gal. Bossy in bed, that had been no problem, but he would have to get his need to command everywhere else but with her. Probably while he was at work.

"I'm good. Wolves don't come out during the daylight, usually."

"What? Find another place to run. There has to be one."

She was startled at the ferocity of his words but tried to laugh it off. "I'm kidding. We don't have many wolves here. Farther north, there are more, but we're on an island. Few mammals swim this far over except on the backside of the island, over the mountain ridge where there is plenty of untouched land for them."

"I know it's wilder here, but I saw there were a few ball fields you could drive to for a course run."

"Too boring. Look, I promise you don't have to worry about me."

"We're still getting used to the area," his voice actually lowered, "but I'm serious about staying safe. That's non-negotiable, sweetheart. I'm not one to make idle statements or commands. And no one disobeys without consequences."

His meaning was clear, and she loved and hated how it made her feel. She was as ready to meet him in the bed for some fun as she was to 'disobey' big time. She met his stare, his gaze penetrated her very soul. She could almost swear it. His possessive tone shook her in the way it wrapped her in warmth. Did he have to hold her stare so intently, and did it have to make her belly jump with excitement every time?

"I told you, I don't do well with orders, Zayden. See you."

"You'll learn." He called after her. "Have a good run and stay on the established paths."

She smiled and wiggled her hand in a backward wave as she ran off. She was slippery at the juncture of her thighs, obviously leaking because it was making her skin feel icky as she ran. Great, another reason to hate running. She wondered if she affected him the same way. It would only be fair.

Later that afternoon, as Alesha was cleaning out flowerbeds, which she enjoyed four months out of the year, the children returned. She set Kami and Kade to carefully picking out the rocks and lining them up. They were serious about their work. A result of living with their father, she was sure. Katrina helped as she spoke.

"People are coming tomorrow to answer all of daddy's questions. But I'm worried he will scare them off or," she lowered her voice, "twins might be too much. We need young and peppy or older with experience, daddy said."

"I thought he'd already hired someone."

"Daddy said it's plan 'C.'"

"I see." She wanted to hug the little girl that was too mature.

Kat looked skeptical. "Daddy needs to lighten up, but he won't, not until he says we have everything in order. That means that he needs a wife, and until then, we need a babysitter."

Alli had had this conversation so often with Katrina that she'd decided not to engage again.

"Daddy's coming, but he needs a wife, so think about it," she repeated. The children ran back to their yard.

"How was your run?"

Still stunned at Kat's persistence, she shrugged. "Horrible. I hate running, but I'm too lazy to find something else to do.

Good though in that there was only one bear, a long way off."
At his look of incredulity, she laughed. "No, really, he was
about a quarter-mile away going along the beach. I was above
him."

"You're lucky. I have a paddle just the right size for naughty
women who put themselves in danger or tease their men about
the same thing."

She was scandalized now. "You don't use that on the children." It was a demanding statement.

"Absolutely not. Both Kat and I have already told you.
However, you protest a lot for a woman who orgasmed when
her man added some strategically timed swats to her ass. I won-
der if I should find a nice leather one to use on a deserving
woman, though. Best of both worlds.

Alli's heart pounded. Zayden stopped talking, but Alesha
couldn't bear to fill in the void. He'd referred to himself as her
man. Then she had the paddle statement to deal with. Her face
was scorching with heat. Zed reached out and touched her hot
skin, sending her belly back to the nationals, this time for som-
ersaulting.

"That excites you, what I said about paddling, maybe not
the paddle itself but the act of swatting your ass. Don't be
ashamed, Alli. We know this about each other. Everyone has
things that excite them. It's who you are, who *we* are together
and if it doesn't harm anyone nor done outside consent, then it
shouldn't be a problem." He grinned at her. "Besides, it's hot to
see your pink bottom and feel the warmth as we make love, and
your orgasms are a sight to behold."

Her embarrassed indignation was loud and clear. "I don't
know what you're talking about."

"Alli, the only thing you reacted to was the paddling state-ment. You said nothing about the relationship part."

"Relationship?"

She could feel her pink bits grow slick, likely turning red with the effect of her arousal. She shrugged and looked at the top button on his shirt and said nothing. There was no need. Heat now engulfed her whole body, and she was sure she was bright red everywhere. It spoke volumes in its betrayal of her inner thoughts.

"Yes, ma'am. I said, in essence, that I was your boyfriend ex-cept I promise you, I'm no one's boy."

"Oh. I definitely know that. Are you sure about the rela-tionship?"

"I'm very sure."

"Me, too, but no paddling."

He gave her a deliciously, wicked smile. "Just strategically timed swats."

"No, I mean..."

"We'll negotiate."

She saw the shadow of his head as he lowered it. She looked into his intense, emotion darkened eyes, waiting for his lips to claim hers. His touch was gently confident, drawing out every bit of her longing. His kiss was needy, demanding, adding raw-ness to his touch, feeding the aching want in her deepest places.

With a tortured groan, he released her mouth, almost wrenched himself from her before taking a labored breath and then a step away, still touching her arms. Reluctantly, Zed re-leased his final physical hold on her. He took another ragged breath.

"I'll be back later for more of this. Much more."

She nodded at his controlled retreat as he turned abruptly and stalked away. What just happened? Should she even be pursuing this when she already had to change her panties whenever he was around? Was she *too* into him? Was there such a thing if she wasn't a stalker or something?

Men are different, she reminded herself. They easily confuse lust with a deeper feeling of love. She wasn't in "like" she was definitely in love. His children seemed to have decided she was the perfect candidate for their father, but what about him? Was he falling in love or lust? Did he get the same unquenchable desire to be skin to skin with her every moment of the day and night? She no longer had any choice. Her heart was committed, and her brain would follow. Would he?

Chapter Eleven

Zayden relaxed with one finger of his favorite scotch whiskey in a cut crystal glass Chrissy had bought him for one Christmas. While sitting in his newly configurated and updated den with its built-in shelves and a big desk, he marveled he was in the home that now belonged to him. He remembered Alesha's expression earlier in the day when she discovered he'd claimed her as his. Zed wasn't sure what she had been thinking before. He'd thought he'd been very clear about where he was headed, not only in their relationship but their future.

Alesha seemed to need it spelled out with no inuendoes, no between-the-lines conversation. She'd been hurt. Her defenses were up even though she was attracted to him. He was fast on his way to loving this woman with his whole being. She fought the capitulation because it made her vulnerable. He would make sure she was confident in where she stood with him. It would allow her to relax and her true feelings to surface. Right now, it was sex, arousal, attraction. Soon it would be love and commitment.

The memory of her gray-blue eyes that sometimes glinted a sliver of sparkle reminded him of his drink. Her powerful gaze held an abundance of stormy emotion, like the strong hints of peat and cherry in his scotch. And like that whiskey, it added depth and richness to the tasting experience. Lingering tastes of the smoky warmth of that liquor glided across the tongue and down one's throat.

The feel of Alli's wet mouth on his body and her forthright efforts to share her life with him overwhelmed Zed sometimes. His need for her, his longing to be all she needed, could devour him if he were not careful. That woman heated his insides to inferno levels. She was worth every careful move he made. He was in this for keeps, and he wouldn't rush anything no matter how many times he had to restrain his libido.

He loved sensual spanking, and he had no doubt Alli did too. Few women were secure enough in themselves to divulge or admit their sensual needs even when it was something so benign as their back ends had nerve endings that created the same biological response as other forms of foreplay.

His life had turned a new page, hell, it had started a new chapter in a new book. This time he wanted to be upfront and thought he'd done a fair job of it so far. If you didn't count that fiasco with the child disclosure part. Fate had dropped this woman in his lap, and you always used the resources at your disposal to meet your goal, no matter how you acquired them.

TODAY, ZED FOUND IT increasingly difficult to keep his concentration in between tasks. All he seemed to do was think about spending time with a free-spirited woman who didn't like taking orders. It would be so much fun teaching her to abide by his orders. She'd not only take his instructions, but Alesha would also take his protection, his tongue, his cock, his hand, oh, yes, so many things. His love. There his wandering brain went again. He stood and walked over to the stack of books. Time to unpack another box.

Early the following morning, Zayden went for his run. After he'd gone his thirty minutes out and stretched it just a little further before covering the miles in reverse, he entered the cul-de-sac sweating but not soaked as the temps were cool compared to Southern Cal. He looked up and saw Alli. His cock, even though it was not thinking of coupling five minutes ago, was staging an uprising of monstrous proportions.

Well, that should answer any question she might have had about his desire for her. Where had his control gone? Ever since embarking on this move and meeting Alesha, his world had shifted. He knew he could get things under control if he could get Alli on board. Now he knew why men with children remarried so quickly. If they didn't, they'd never get any relief, emotionally or physically. He laughed at his own dramatics.

Alesha stood up from her stretching and stared at Zed while he cooled down by walking back and forth in front of her. "Wow, um, you're out early."

He heard her words but watched her eyes on his crotch. Yep, no hiding that truth. His breathing more relaxed, he bent down to retie her shoes as he answered her as naturally as if she belonged to him and he had the right. In his eyes, she did belong to him, and therefore, he did have every right.

"You're going to twist your ankle if you don't keep these tight enough. And this is the time I always do PT. When we are in our normal routine, that is."

"Thank you, but if they're too tight, it's uncomfortable. Shoes are uncomfortable enough already because I'm a barefoot kinda girl."

"However, if they are not tight enough, you don't have adequate support, and you'll twist your ankles. I don't think you live in a barefoot climate."

He knew he sounded dictatorial, but why deny who he was? Alli was wrong about one assumption. Zed expected people to follow his orders. Only in the military world. His family had taught him early on that in the civilian world, it was hit and miss. More misses than hits.

"Oh, I'm barefoot every chance I get. I've never twisted my ankle from running, and I don't tie them this tight." She leaned down to retie her shoes more comfortably.

Zayden put his hand on her arm. "Will you at least compromise? Tie them tighter than you had them but not as tight as I tied them."

Alicia looked at him for a long moment and then nodded. "I can compromise."

ALLI WANTED TO TELL him to leave her footwear alone, but when he flashed that brilliant smile, she was a goner. She immediately envisioned him with pilot sunshades and an infectious arrogant grin. She felt that damn flush again. The reaction no longer shocked her. This man elicited that type of jolting response from her with just conversation and a smile. He shamefully took her desire to push against his control and swallowed it whole with just a look. He'd done it every time. Was she doomed? Oh, hell, yes, but she refused to go down without a fight.

As they stood in the chilled post-dawn air that threatened a downpour, Zayden stood straight and tall. He seemed to have a tight rein on his demeanor even at the end of his run. His athletic shorts and T-shirt showcased his muscular build, and his skin was sweaty. She wanted to touch him, and to her horror, she found her hand beginning to reach forward before she detoured its direction to rub the palms on her shorts.

She recalled his naked splendor. He didn't look like a bodybuilder, but he did look like a man who took his exercise seriously. This was the beginning of his session that, according to Zed, included weights, pull-ups, sit-ups and assorted other nightmarish endeavors. She slid her eyes back up his body to meet his amused look. Then he shrugged.

"I don't have a choice, I have to stay fit for the job and equally important, raising three rug rats alone makes me head rat. I have to be ready for anything. Is there a complaint?"

"You know there isn't. Well, maybe just one. I want to touch you all over, and yet, I don't get near as much sexy time as I want. I need you, Zed."

Gone was the easygoing man replaced by the serious Zayden. "You have the key, Alesha. Tonight. There is only one acceptable answer, and you know what that is, now tie your shoes."

"I did."

He placed his finger in the space between her foot and the shoe. "Again, they are too loose."

"No, I—"

"Unless you want to feel my hand on that shapely ass, you'd better learn to do as you're told when it's for your own good."

"I told you I—"

"Don't take orders well, and I told you, you'll learn." He ran his finger down her cheek. "Please?"

Alli sighed and nodded. She re-tied the shoes. He made her melt, and her heart now beat like a dance drum. It was time to begin again. The first place to start: the bedroom.

"Are you officially all moved in now?"

"Just one last thing to move in."

"Oh?"

"Yeah, but I'm working on it, and I'm sure it won't be too long now. Tonight, in fact, I'm trying out the fit. All night."

Alli's face heated. "Oh. But I'm so close, I don't have to move in. That has to be better."

"For whom?"

"Everyone."

"You're wrong, but I'll settle for you warming my bed at night, for now." He looked at the house. "I'm waiting for the kids to wake up because I have things to do later this morning. I could put it off as late as mid-afternoon, but that's about it. I'm used to having help with them, you see, and I'm learning how much help I had."

"After my run, I'm not doing anything else today. I can watch the kids."

"I couldn't ask you to do that."

"Please, Zed. There can't be any conversation about moving ahead before the kids and I establish where I fit into their life. We'll have breakfast and kick a ball around or something. I know how to keep children occupied."

"No beach until I've gone over the rules with them."

"No trouble. Looks like rain, anyway."

"It always looks like rain."

"Not true," she laughed. She waved as she took off. Later she walked over and released Zed to finish his errands.

The twins happily accepted and devoured their morning snack. No sweet treat for these military offspring. She had already assembled their yogurt and fruit. Zed was a big one for schedules and plans. She, however, wasn't except for her classes. In her private life, she was a freedom seeker. Freedom from as many conventions as she could have.

Living in a secluded cul-de-sac made playing more fun. Alli was sitting on the front porch, watching when the phone rang.

"Do not leave from the front of the house. I'll be right back." Katrina was creating a masterpiece on her tablet and merely nodded when she heard Alesha.

Coming back after taking the message from one of Zayden's guys, Alli looked around. Katrina hadn't moved a muscle, and the twins were... gone! She looked and called everywhere until she heard a screech and Kami crying. Up on the top of the detached garage were two little five-year-old's and her heart stopped.

"Okay, okay, hold on. How did you guys get up there?"

Kade said in a shaky voice, "the ladder."

Looking around, she located the rickety wooden ladder and had to talk herself calmer. She wasn't deathly afraid of heights, but they did bother her. The children were hugging the edge of the rooftop cap, and Alli could hardly breathe. If they let go, they might slide down the roof slant and stop, or they might fall off.

"Katrina, I need you now." Alesha had tried to instill that commanding voice that came naturally to Zed. It worked. Katrina came running.

"Okay, I need you to hold on to the ladder when Kaden and Kami come down. Got that?"

Katrina kept her eyes firmly on Alli and then the ladder. She nodded. Alli climbed up without thinking. She made quick work of getting the crying Kami down first and then Kade. As she began to follow him to safety, he yelled up to her, "My ball is still there."

She was barefooted as usual, so the debris on the roof from countless storms made walking to the other side difficult. Her adrenalin was receding fast, leaving her high and dry. Grabbing the ball, she leaned over slightly to toss it off the roof. At just that moment, an eagle who obviously needed glasses swooped too close, scaring her out of a decade of life as she slid down to the gutter, which was luckily sturdy and well-attached.

The children screamed and yelled at the eagle. Trying to calm them down, Alli eased her body inch by treacherous inch to the ladder. Katrina was still at her duty station and looking as serious as her father ever had as she watched Alli gratefully climbed down. Alesha praised Katrina and gave the twins a good talking to about dangerous situations, eliciting a promise they would never do that again. She decided the outside games were over.

When Zayden returned, Alli exited quickly, hoping the story would lose something in the retelling. Unfortunately, her hopes were unrealized. Her phone rang soon after she got home.

"Hi."

"What the hell were you thinking to climb up on the roof like that?"

"Um, to get the children. Or maybe you would have preferred that I left them there on the roof, scared, crying, and holding on for dear life?"

"No, I would have preferred that you had watched them closer, dammit."

"What the hell, Zayden Wellesley! You listen to me, you overgrown bully. I told the children not to leave the front yard. I answered the phone and took a message which, if you're in the kitchen, you'll be looking at on the whiteboard. When I returned, they were up on the roof. That fast."

Zed was silent. "Okay," he said calmer, "I believe that, but they said you went back for the ball."

"Well, yeah. That's why they climbed up in the first place."

"And almost fell off."

"An eagle thought I was going to threaten his nest. That's all. I didn't fall off."

"But you did slide down the roof."

"Yes, but–"

"Almost off the roof."

"Okay but–"

"I'm coming over."

The door soon opened forcefully. Zayden didn't even knock.

Alli looked up from her project on the kitchen table. "I'm fine. Zed–"

Without a word, Zayden scooped Alli up and headed for the bedroom. The door slammed behind them, and he turned the lock. "Strip."

"What?" Alli had no time to say another word as he was stripping her as though her clothes were on fire.

The absolute next thought was *he's spanking me!*

"Zed, wait, stop, ow."

Zed laid her over his propped knee and quickly picked up a staccato rhythm, his hand landing hard and fast on the whole of her rear end. "I could have lost you over a ball. Alesha Campbell, I cannot, will not allow you to jeopardize your life over something so inane as a ball. If I ever, and I mean ever, find you risking your safety for no good reason, we will be doing this with my belt. Am I understood?"

Alli's face was covered in her shed tears, She heard him, but her throat was clogged with even more tears. She managed to croak out a sorrowful "yes," and Zed immediately stood her upright.

"Thank God you're safe."

His hands began to remove his clothes. Clued into what was going to happen next, Alesha started on Zed's clothes to help the process along, but she was obviously going at less than lightning speed, which was too slow for him.

"Zed–ahh..." her words were cut off by his mouth that covered her nipple and surrounding breast. He sucked hard.

"I cannot believe you put yourself in danger for a damn ball." His mouth came down over hers, crashing into her lips and extracting a punishment of their own. He was devouring her, and she met him heat for heat.

She panted as his mouth released hers and headed south over her tummy, nuzzling her muff. Then he invaded her fleshy parts beneath. "God, Zed, I can't..."

"You had better hold on, my naughty girl. I'm coming in, and you're going to come all over my cock."

He reared up and entered her hard, his pelvis slammed hers. In and out, the rhythm was strong and predictable. "I'm getting close."

Zed turned her around to her hands and knees, ass up high, hands clutching the spread. He never once disengaged his cock from her sheath. Alli didn't have one clue how he could have done it, but her brain was fogged with lust.

"Do. Not. Let. Go. No coming until I say so."

He slapped her ass several times, giving equal attention to each cheek. Each time his hand connected with her backside was more intense than the last. Alli couldn't believe the raging inferno those swats stoked in her after his furious spanking. Soon she would be consumed. He leaned down to put just the right amount of pressure on her button that controlled the nerve center when she became almost frantic in her begging.

"Now, baby, let's find your happy place."

His elongated grunt met her panting squeal of release. Fast, dirty, done. And she couldn't have been more pleased with the outcome but not in a relaxed way. It was more of a burst of expended energy, leaving a low level of anticipation of more. She wasn't satiated by any means. She wanted more but no strength to repeat the play.

When her breathing had calmed somewhat, Alli noticed Zed hadn't said anything. "You okay?"

"I am now. You scared years off my life, woman."

"Are you kidding me? I had no choice but to do what I did. You only heard the story after you knew the outcome. I didn't have that luxury."

"I should have spanked you harder."

"No, that was quite enough. You have to know that I wouldn't have done it if I'd had a choice, Zed."

"I know baby." He kissed her gently. "That old ladder is gone. I took it out of the garage to take to the dump but forgot about it. I'll replace it, not that you'll be using it."

"Thanks, but I've got my own." He didn't reply. "Um, can we do this again?"

"Alli," he asked quietly, "Are you on birth control?"

"No, why... damn."

"I was so frustrated and desperate to be inside you I didn't protect. It's okay. I promise it will be okay."

"Zed, it's fine. I don't think anything will happen, but if it does, I can handle it."

"We. We can handle it."

"Can I have a sleepover tonight?"

"Hell yeah. I'd prefer to have you every night."

Alli wondered if she didn't prefer it as well.

ZED LOADED UP THE KIDS for a library run and to get groceries. He'd handle his chores around the house and settle the kids first, then it would be time to work on his training manual. He'd been working on it since accepting the job, but the rest of life had been so intrusive, he hadn't had much time to concentrate on it. The time that he would need to put it into play was fast approaching. His intention was to spend most of his days and likely evenings, finalizing it.

Zed hadn't seen Alli since early this morning when she went home as he left for his run. He'd been pretty rough with her yesterday, but last night, they made the sweetest love. She was so willing when he seemed to need to cherish her. She'd cried. He ached for her to sleep with him every night.

"Daddy, daddy, there's Alli. Stop, she's hurt." That had him putting on the brakes.

"Where Kami?" All three kids pointed behind them, and as they opened their door, he barked at them to close it. Echoes of "yes, daddy," were heard before he opened, exited, and jogged around to the side of the road.

"Hey, sweetheart, what happened?" He went down on his haunches in front of her to stop her limping progress. He reached for her foot when she stopped.

"Don't touch it... me. Zed, I'm fine, really. Nothing's wrong."

"Alesha, what happened and do not tell me *nothing*. I don't do well with lies or brush offs."

"Fine." She put her fists on her hips, and if Zed wasn't in protector mode, he would have laughed out loud. "I twisted my ankle because I loosened my shoelaces because I was mad at you."

"Excuse me?"

"I was mad that I tried to tie it the way you did because you told me to. I don't like that I want to please you. That's all. No big deal. Now go away."

"Why didn't you call me?"

He reached for her foot anyway, and she yanked it out of his reach, hissing in her ill-advised movement. He swatted her exposed thigh. They both stopped and stared at each other. He might as well go all in because he'd claimed her for good in his bed and hers.

"Alesha, answer me."

"Because," she yelled. "My cell doesn't work in this section of the road."

"Then you don't run this way alone again. Got it?"

"It wouldn't have mattered, anyway."

"What? Why?" he'd released her foot gently and stood, keeping a hand on her waist to steady her.

"Because I don't have your damn house number."

"What? But my cell... Damn. Why don't you... right." He nodded. He'd gotten a new cell number and provider yesterday on his errands because his provider didn't cover Island Life, Alaska. His house phone was obviously new as well. "Your foot is swollen but no more damage than that. I meant it when I said you needed to tighten the laces. Then to loosen them because you're mad is juvenile. I think we're close enough and familiar enough for you to understand that if you don't have a good reason to disobey my directives, then you'll have earned my displeasure and the response."

"What are you saying, exactly?"

"You need discipline. You need someone who cares enough about you to hold you accountable for stubborn responses. That's me and only me. It's what you need today, a good spanking, but the kids are watching."

"What if I don't, won't, allow it? Yesterday was—"

"Yesterday was fear-driven. It was many things but not typically how I administer spankings. Remember consent and implied consent? You're mine now. You still have a choice, but there is implied consent. Your consent is implied when we have engaged in things you've not been against historically. Swats, for instance, or my protection. But you don't want a choice, do you, sweetheart?" Zayden picked Alesha up and carried her to his SUV. "You want me to take care of you, show you how special you are, but you fight it because you think you shouldn't want it. That your desires aren't socially acceptable, politically correct. That they make you vulnerable."

Sitting Alli in the empty front seat of his car, he gave her no chance to respond. Zed leaned close, so his words were only for her. "When are you going to quit allowing the vocal crazies of the world to dictate what is enjoyable for you? What you want?" He stepped back and spoke in normal tones. "I have to get a few things at the grocer's, so you'll have to wait a few more minutes. Then I'll get you home."

Zed drove to the store, and the kids began to pile out. "Don't we want to take Alli in too, daddy?"

He looked over at Alesha. "No, her foot hurts, and she needs some quiet time."

"Oh," said Kade sounding as wise as his older sister.

When the group came out of the grocery store, Alesha was gone. "Damn," he said under his breath. "Okay. Get in, guys."

The car ride home was quiet. Zed had enough of the cat and mouse games because he didn't have time for any more messing around. If Alli needed more time, she would have to say because he needed either the green light or the cold shoulder. He wanted to heat her bottom to a red-hot glowing sphere and then make fierce love to her. She frustrated him and sent his cock into orbit.

He wanted her in his home, his bed and his life for good. She would either agree to at least go forward, or he'd be taking a lot of cold showers. A cab was pulling away from Alli's door, and Zayden forced himself to take the groceries and children home. He called the babysitter.

An hour later, he left the kids with Samantha and took wine, two plates of early supper, pain reliever, ice packs and an ace bandage over with him. He would declare his desires but not abruptly and coarsely. Alesha either accepted him, or she didn't, but he would know. It would hurt if she rejected him, but somehow, he didn't think she would. Zayden hoped his gut was right. He'd misread a few things lately, and it put him off his game.

Zayden knocked, but when she didn't answer, he opened the side door facing his house because he knew it was always unlocked. It would be another area of discussion, but not today. Dropping his supplies on the kitchen table, he continued until he heard her unrestrained sniffles. In the living room, curled up on the couch, was a crying Alli. Zed's heart seized.

Without saying a word, he picked her up from the over-stuffed sofa she'd folded herself into and sat down, settling her in his lap, being careful of her ankle. She looked up into his face, hers streaked with the tracks of her salty tears. She tried to speak, but he shushed her. Her tears continued as she leaned into his chest as he wordlessly rocked, and crooned, and kissed.

"I'm sorry." Her voice sounded muffled and soggy.

"Hmm, baby, what are you sorry about?" his gentle words were almost lost in the resumption of her tears. He hummed and held her until they subsided again.

Hiccups and stuttering breaths interspersed her voice as she tried to speak. "I don't know exactly. For getting mad at you, for crying all over your shirt, for taking off without saying anything at the store, for wanting what you can give me, for wanting you." She sniffed. "For not thanking you."

"Oh, sweetheart, these are all things that need no apology." He grinned. "This time."

Her watery laugh made Zed's gut clench again, his groin raced blood to his shaft, and he could feel it thicken and lengthen in response.

"I don't know what has come over me. I'm an educated woman, but ever since I laid eyes on you, heard your voice, you're all I can think about. Now that you live next door, I'm doomed. And my hidden desires, those little quirky things that I like, that you give me make me sizzle with need. And you don't even make me feel bad about them."

"It's my charm." They both chuckled, but Zayden grew serious. "We need to talk. I've brought us food and a bottle of wine. It will have to do for tonight."

"Oh, we can't. What about the children? You have to go home. You left them alone. Go." She tried to push him away as she attempted to climb out of his lap, but he didn't budge. He didn't appear worried.

"No, stop and listen to me. I called the babysitter and said it was to help her get used to the children and vice-versa. To answer any questions that pop up before I'm on a different island. You must start trusting me, trust my instincts, or you'll find this a long, hot assed summer."

"But—"

"Let's get our dinner and talk."

Chapter Twelve

Alli watched as Zayden picked her up and carried her as though she were a child. Alesha was uncomfortable being carried, and she did worry about over-taxing him. He was probably only a few years her senior, and well-toned, but she was sure he was feeling the strain.

"I know you make it look easy, but I weigh considerably more than most men could handle, and you've done it twice now. I can hobble just fine, so you can put me down. And for your information, I'm not running, for exercise, anymore. I hated it before this, and now I'm so over it. I'll do something else."

He made a dissenting grumbling sound in his chest, and she stared into a face that showed definite displeasure. "You work hard at earning your punishment, I can tell you that." He said with a shake of his head.

Misunderstanding his upset, she offered. "I could swim, but the water is kinda cold. I'll figure out something, promise."

"Sweetheart, I couldn't care less what you choose to get in some exercise."

"Oh, I thought it upset you about the exercise, seeing as you are... well... into that."

"Safety, sweetheart. Worrying about how much you weigh, how much I can handle is not a good use of your energy, especially since I'm not happy you left the car when I told you to stay, becoming hurt because of your obstinance, and stranded because of your lack of planning. Those are areas that are causing me some concern and giving me itchy palm syndrome."

He raised an eyebrow and nodded once, almost daring her to refute his words. But she couldn't. She wanted him to claim her in a very real way as he'd tried to do. Could he see the heat rise in her face? If not, he should. She was embarrassed and so turned on she wiggled in his arms before he sat her in a dining chair.

Alli watched out of her peripheral vision as his hand slid over her cheek, her lips tickled as his thumb traced the delicate skin making her sensual juices flowed. He finished the ice wrap on her ankle and placed a pillow on the seat of another chair to prop her foot.

"You have the cutest blush I've ever seen. It makes me diamond hard. We'll deal with everything later, including your blush and my hard-on. Right now, I'm going to heat the plates in the microwave for a few minutes to get them piping again and then we will talk."

The best Alli could do was nod. She vibrated with need. As Zayden left the room, she had no doubt why she was falling in love with this infuriating man. It was because he took their relationship, her feelings and his responsibilities so seriously. He'd claimed her in so many ways, how could she not allow him in her life, permanently? Maybe tonight they would make the breakthrough she needed to give into him. She arranged herself in the chair better and lifted her hair to let air flow along her damp neck. A whisper of lips pressed against her nape and then gone. She shivered and let her hair drop.

A plate appeared before her on the table along with a napkin, silverware and an empty wine glass. She watched as Zayden did the same for himself and then stepped out of the room only to return quickly with a chilled bottle of white wine.

"White for fish, but if you like, I see you have a red in the cabinet."

"No, white's fine."

They ate for a few silent moments enjoying the excellent fare. The fish wasn't overcooked, the rice pilaf fluffy. Zed brought salad, and she ate it, but the broccoli was going to sit on her plate. She didn't do anything else green but lettuce leaves and celery and neither of those bare.

"Don't forget to eat your broccoli."

"How did you know?"

"Excuse me?"

"How did you know that I was not going to eat it?"

Zed stopped chewing and looked up to show his confusion at the question. Then he shrugged. "I usually read people pretty well."

"I don't like broccoli."

"Then, eat all the salad."

"Except the bell peppers." Zed laid down his fork and leaned back to contemplate her, and she hated it. "Quit staring, it isn't polite."

"Sometimes, it's like dealing with another..."

"Another what? Child? Were you about to compare me to a child because I'm not eating what you want me to eat? News flash. Women, defined as grown-up females, can choose whatever they want to eat. And you know why? Because we are *grown up*."

She started to push her chair back, and Zed was up and out of his seat in a flash, stopping her motion before she could process he'd moved. "Damn it. Why can't I ever win with you?"

He squatted in front of her chair. "Because I'm right and you don't want to win, you want me to settle the ground, end your insecurities. Alesha Campbell, I'm seriously falling in love with you. I'm not misreading my feelings. I know what loving someone feels like. You might not want to hear that, but it's the truth. And because of that one little fact, I'm always going to worry about what you eat or don't eat, your sleep, your safety, and a whole gambit of crap you might not feel prepared to deal with, but you will. Why? Because you need me to need you. You want my love and protection, and you're acting like a petulant child because your needs aren't being met." He reached and touched her cheek. "And you're having a hard time asking for what you want." He kissed her softly. "Now, am I going to get agreement or are you going to continue being a brat to force me to deal with you as proof of how much you mean to me?"

She scrunched up her nose and twisted her lips ruefully. "I really don't like broccoli or bell peppers."

"Understood. Anything else?"

"I like everything else you brought."

"And?"

"And why do you always have to be right, damn it?"

"Are we back to that again?"

She chuckled. "You make it hard to win a fight with you. That annoys me. A lot."

"Good." He grazed his finger over her cheek and stood. "I don't want you to fight me on the important stuff, but on the contents of your salad, complain away."

She laughed and sniffed as she wiped a few escaping tears.

"I love to hear your laugh."

"I know guys think it's annoying."

Zayden looked surprised and then irritable. "Who told you that?"

Shrugging, she didn't respond. It was a little disconcerting to realize that not all guys thought that, but she'd heard it more than once. That he didn't feel that way made her fall for him a little more. As if she needed another reason.

"Alli honey, you need to listen to me. I don't care what anyone else says, you're adorable, funny, intelligent, and the perfect blend of sweet and spicy for me. I don't give a flying fuck what anyone else thinks, and I don't want you to give them another thought. *They* don't matter. *We* matter. The family I want to share with you, create with you, matters."

She nodded, too choked to speak. Zed stood dropped a warm, hungry kiss on her upturned lips and sat back in his chair. They concentrated on their food a few moments before she tried to speak again.

"I'm sorry... I didn't know I had so many insecurities." She shook her head, releasing a deep breath. "So, what did you want to talk about?" Another diversion, she knew, but it was one he accepted.

"I can't just do things like I used to; otherwise, I would have done. I mean, years ago, when I liked a woman or wanted to pursue her, I would take her out to eat, bed her, and when one or both of us was no longer interested in the relationship, we would move on. Whether I like to admit it or not, I was young and stupid once, and as cocky and horny as the next guy.

But then I met Chrissy, and everything changed. We married, and before we knew it, Kat had joined the party."

He took another bite and grinned. "Now, it's different, I'm not young or stupid, but I'm still horny. I'm also starting with three little pieces of demanding baggage and a load of responsibility that I can't afford to be neglectful of both at home and professionally. It makes pursuing a woman in the way that she deserves difficult."

"They are adorable pieces of baggage, and I understand. So why tell me?"

"Alli, I told you I want you. I've lusted after a few women since we lost Chrissy, but not drawn to them. I didn't feel more than the passing protectiveness I have for most women. The spark you bring excites me, and I crave it, but I don't want to battle over supremacy at home." His shrug was one of acceptance of who he was, a protector, bossy, alpha male, and Alli could see him easily leading a pack of hungry but respectful wolves.

Time to own her feelings and accept him. "I'm past the 'like you' stage." She lifted her eyes to his. "Way past."

"Well, then I guess that answers my first question. As I was saying, I don't have the luxury of going the normal route. I need to factor in the children. I think we have that covered as well because Kat is working a pretty strong angle to get us alone or at least together. She has no idea we spent quality time while I was up here last month. Not sure just how much a nine-year-old knows, but I'm beginning to have visions of long nights waiting up for her dates to end."

He paused, and Alli instinctively knew Zed had more to say. She took another bite and waited. He finished his dinner and put his fork down. Reaching for his wine glass, he drained the rest and refilled it before taking another small sip.

"I'm a hard man to be with, Alli. I have control issues that are fine for me as a dad and as a commander, but others are sometimes put off, especially women who don't want a take-charge kind of guy in their life. I won't apologize for it. It is something that I needed in my marriage, but I gladly adjusted to what and how much Chrissy could handle. It was enough for me to feel satisfied, but..."

"But not fulfilled?"

He shook his head. "Chrissy fulfilled me. I loved being married to her, it's just, things are different now, and I want it all. I know it's selfish, but I want dominance in more than mowing the grass when I'm home or being the bad guy to the salesman at the door. Don't get me wrong, we were very happy and if she hadn't... well, if there hadn't been that car accident on her way home from watching me do a jump, then we would still be married and living the life we built with no regrets."

Alesha put her fork down and pushed her plate away. "In my previous relationships, I didn't have enough diversity, or experience in my sexuality to understand that if you have to keep things to yourself, then you were with the wrong person. I hid so much of what I craved in a relationship because I didn't want to rock the boat. I didn't know what I was missing, but it was something. That being said, I didn't think I was unhappy." She took another sip of wine. "So now that you have another opportunity, you want things different. What does that mean exactly, Zed?"

"It means I can't go as slow as you deserve. It means I have to be upfront and honest. I will be the leader of my family, my romantic relationship, my marriage, and not just in the bedroom. Since I no longer gallivant all over God's green earth at the drop of a hat, I'll be home most nights. Now, I'll expect more acceptance of my place in the home. And since I've been the sole parent these last years, I know I want to take a more active part in my family's lives. Not just the sporting side or the boss of the world, like Kami calls me, but a full part of the decision-making process on the big things."

"I understand your words, Zed, but what does it mean exactly? What does it mean for me? Us?"

Zed hesitated, and then, to her astonishment, he grabbed plates and took them into the kitchen. He came out with the red bottle of wine, a corkscrew, and walked past her.

"Stay there."

Instead, she grabbed the glasses and tried to follow. He was back quickly. "Now this right here is what I'm talking about. You need to trust me enough to listen to me."

She could feel his arm around her belly as he took the glasses from her and sat them down. Leaning her over his forearm, he landed four hard swats on her ass.

"Ow!"

"Grab the glasses." Stunned at his change in demeanor, she complied with her sex weeping, her head swearing. Lifting her, he walked to the sofa. Arranging her comfortably, placing the wine glasses on the side table, he sat beside her, pouring more wine before pulling her close to his chest. He handed her a glass. For the second time, Zed drained his own before setting it on the table again.

"Okay, so here goes. First, I'm a rather old-fashioned man in that I'm the head of my house and have, on occasion, spanked my woman. I do like order and control in my life, which includes at home. It's who I am. I can assure you that I will occasionally give you a few swats, like today, but if I do, while I am intent on getting a message across, I also intend on giving you mind-blowing sex afterward, if possible."

"I'm not a child."

"Nope, there is no doubt about that fact. You're perfect for me. I like giving my girl sexy spankings when we make love. It just makes me harder. When I'm with you, everything makes me hot. If I haven't misread things, I believe you have demonstrated you like it too."

"Like might be too strong a word. I don't want you to treat me like an errant child."

"I would never disrespect you or allow anyone else to do that. Please understand, it isn't as big a deal as I'm making it. If I'm really upset about something, we talk. I've found withholding your orgasms work better. I try never to be a yeller at home. In the field, on the job, I'm a completely different man. I have to be."

"You have a firm hand, buster."

He grinned and shrugged but didn't apologize. "But you did like it."

"I plead the fifth. Okay, what else?"

Her tummy had the crazies right now, and all she could do was say a few words at one time. Zayden seemed to relax. Lucky him.

"I'm bossy, and that wouldn't change. I would respect your authority with the children and in our life. Your domain is your domain. I'd never embarrass you, but let me assure you that if I give you directions if I say something does or doesn't happen based on my protecting you or the kids, I'm serious. I can't keep you safe if you don't trust me to do just that. You prove that by allowing my authority when necessary."

Still tingling from the implication of his words, her tender bits were slippery in arousal. Alli said, "Okay, but what if it isn't dangerous, you just think it is?"

"Convince me. But in the heat of the moment, there is no discussion. I compromise all the time but not the safety of the people I love, those that mean something to me. My team, co-workers, my family trust my word, and so will my woman."

He waited before continuing. Alesha's mind was churning away with Kaden's words: My Woman.

"Alesha, what are you thinking?"

"That I'm scared. I think I want it, but the reality might be too much for me."

"We're living the reality now. Predominately." They both knew the final pieces. She hadn't moved in, and he hadn't proposed.

"In my past relationship, he was demeaning and demanding as though that gave him the control. It was all about him, and I saw that later. Not like you. With you," Alli shrugged, "You're relaxed. You do it quietly. I hear you by your manner, not your noise. Usually."

"Consent has to be on both sides in everything that intimate. I'm glad it didn't work out because it gives me a chance with you. Are you ready to take it?"

"Yes, I'm ready. I think we can give each other a chance. More than a chance."

"No secrets, no lies to save feelings, whether you like something or not, you're to say so, and I promise to do the same. We can't build trust in any other way. Deal?"

"Deal."

"One more question."

"Mmm, okay."

"Are we good with the little swats earlier?"

She grinned. "A kiss would be nice. But does that mean I get some great sex now?"

"Thank God. I want to do so much more but with your ankle..." He hesitated before continuing. "It might kill me, but we'll have to wait and see what you look like tomorrow."

Zayden leaned down, his outer arm bracing himself, hand positioned near her cheek as he came in close for the kiss that started light and teasing but soon turned into much more. His loving was tender, then demanding. Plundering then short and teasing. The tantalizing kiss seemed to go on forever. Finally, she heard her own moans turn to whimpers of need, her body sliding against his in a desperate attempt to fulfill a wanton desire. The deep need to satisfy and be satisfied burned in rampaging flames threatening to consume them in its rage. Zayden growled but lifted his head and leaned away.

"I'm a man of my word, sweetheart, and you should get set up in bed. You can read or watch TV or something, but except for a bathroom run, you keep your ankle elevated, iced, and wrapped. I should have changed this ice wrap sooner."

"What? You have got to be kidding me. You can't start and not finish it, that's inhumane."

"I said we wouldn't."

"I don't care. I don't hurt so bad that I can't have sex. Zayden..."

"Tomorrow. I told you withheld orgasms were good punishments for you."

After Zayden carried Alli upstairs, he supervised her changing and made sure she was set up before he turned to leave. "Don't get up. I'll be back after I get the kids to sleep. Could be nine-thirty, but I'll be back unless you call me sooner. And Alli? This is one of those protection situations. I'm not a bully. I'm taking care of you."

His phone rang at just that moment, and after looking at the caller ID, his whole demeanor changed. Just the strength of tone and the authority it carried thrilled her.

"Commander Wellesley here." He looked into her eyes and pointed to the bed. She zinged at his gesture, and the cream flowed. Yep, she had it bad. Zed left the bedroom, and she heard the front door shut firmly.

It was nine, and Alli was hungry. Dinner had been early. Zed had said not to get up, but her foot didn't throb any longer, and she was an adult. She'd just tell him she felt better and wanted something to eat if he came back too soon. She loved that her bedrooms were upstairs except in cases like this. Ugh. She hated that she would have to maneuver the steps. He'd said to call him, but he had to get the kids to sleep. She'd have done it alone before he came into her life. Besides, she would get back to bed before Zed returned.

Sandwich and a bottle of water in hand, she tried to walk up the stairs, but that wasn't going to work, so she sat on the third step and began to go up as she'd come down, on her butt. She was almost to the top when she heard Zed come in the back door. Alli looked up just in time to see her new man that she had said she would listen to when he was trying to keep her safe, rounding the corner. He stopped and crossed his arms over his immense expanded chest and stood with his legs spread. A little like the muscle man on that cleaning commercial. There was no smile on her version.

Trying to act like it wasn't a big deal, she attempted to continue. "Stop. Do not move." Taking the steps two at a time, he snatched her up from her position and carried her like she weighed much less than she did. Once on the landing, he rearranged her and tightened his grip. He laid a searing smack on her ass and then massaged it. A groan of arousal tumbled from her lips.

He kissed her gently. "God, I love your ass." His tone firmed. "Baby, what did I tell you? You need to learn to follow orders.".

"Cut it out, Zed. I was hungry."

"I made sure you had your phone. Why didn't you call?"

"Because you have the kids. It was important for you to do your nighttime routine with them, and I knew you might have had work with that call you got. Because I'm not a dependent type of person. Besides, I'm not in the Navy, and I don't think I'm a follower."

"Everyone is a follower if the leader is competent enough."

"Are you a competent leader, Commander? Not one to remind the rest of the dog team that if they aren't the leader, then the view is always the same? His ass."

He laughed at that. "No, not usually anyway."

Her voice softened. "I'm worried if I put my trust in you, and you don't turn out to be the guy I think you are, or you don't want me, then it will break me."

"Oh, sweetheart, I'm the best type of leader, and I have already decided that there is only going forward with you. You'll never get rid of me now."

"I still don't think I'm a follower, and I know I don't take orders."

"Good to know, because I don't do well with those who blindly follow either, but when the one in front has your best interest at heart, it's the only sensible course of action. Now let's get you back to bed. I have a serious conversation I want to have with you."

Alli worried about what it was he wanted to talk about. He'd swatted her butt again but gently, more of a caress. She was putty in his hands. His touch made her so hot and bothered that it wouldn't take much to fire her rockets.

"How's the ankle, really?"

"Not stairs good, obviously, but not throbbing. I think I'll be fine in the morning."

"Right, so tonight, it's all about making you feel good and tired, so you can sleep."

"Mmm, I do like that idea."

"Thought you would."

"And what can I do for *you*?"

He plucked her nipple. "Lay there and take it."

THE NEXT MORNING, ALLI woke deliciously rested and still sated after Zed's lovemaking. Even though she begged, he never took her but allowed her to return the favor. She still felt the buzz from his gentle massage and fervent kisses that pushed all orderly thought far from her mind. Alli thought she would never stop climaxing from his tongue and fingers. She reciprocated even though he denied she needed to do it. It took her by surprise when pleasuring him heightened her arousal and brought on another orgasm slamming into her right after he climaxed.

Alli had never really enjoyed oral sex either performing it or receiving it. With Chad, it was almost a duty, but with Zed, it was a heady treat. From the moment she had taken him in her mouth, had felt his retracted ball sac, felt his cock grow, she knew she would never hesitate again.

Zed had small grunts and noises of appreciation that helped her understand why her little squeals were such a turn on to him. As he got close to his release, Zed took her head in his hands and bracketed her, holding her in one position while he pumped in and out of her eager mouth. She'd gagged.

"Relax, honey. It should help." He continued his rhythm. "If you want, we can stop."

She shook her head. She concentrated on relaxing just that little bit more, and it was fine. Her nails scraped his sac and then dug into his flexing glutes. Alli was shocked when she felt her own release again as she was pleasuring him. Win-win.

Later, as Zed was redressing, Alli asked how he got such a defined sex line.

"A what?"

She ran her fingers over his obliques that formed the sexy "V." He shivered. "Your sex lines. You know, this 'v.'" She ran her fingers along the outline of his Adonis Belt.

He grinned. "Hard work. It's a byproduct of working out. Part of the core strength building we do in PT. Good to know you think it's sexy."

"Hmm, well, keep it up because I think I'm in love with the result."

"You are, huh? What happens when I'm old and gray and long out of the Navy?"

"Oh, I'll find something else to love and look at the pictures from your hunky powerhouse days and reminisce."

"Is that right?"

"Oh, yeah. But for now, no taking your shirt off in public. I don't want to go to jail for protecting what's mine."

He laughed. "It might be hard to explain to the trainees that my woman was the person they had to be careful of, not me."

"Could happen."

He laughed and kissed her deeply. "Won't, though. I have ways to handle interfering women."

"Women?"

"You, smart ass. I have lots of ways, including a paddle that is just made to redden saucy rear ends like yours."

"Mmm, I might consider it. Does it still come with a side of sex? Yes, please."

"Brat." His kiss was as invading as it was claiming. She sighed as he left to go home. That was the best way to spend an hour.

Alli had fallen asleep right away and had all sorts of naughty, hot dreams featuring her Navy Commander. She could listen to her gut as well as Zayden could his. Hers was saying things were going to change for the better, and she was ready. No more just dreaming of Zayden and hoping to get a little part of him. No more guessing if they were right together. She didn't care about losing her solitude if it meant there'd be no separation from him. No, things were definitely about to change.

Chapter Thirteen

Z ed started the grill while the children ran excitedly around him. He leaned over and kissed Alli's lips lightly, maintaining their relationship in public but on a low key scale. Mostly for the children's sake, but they didn't seem to need extra care as much as the adults. If anyone had checked Zayden's room nightly at about eleven, they would have gotten a real education on how low key they actually were. Alli smiled hesitantly up at Zed. They'd hired two sitters to keep the children entertained when the adults arrived for the Fourth of July barbeque. They used Alli's house as the daycare.

"Are you still nervous about meeting these guys?" Alli shrugged. "Don't be. They're nearer to your age except one, and he's married. Several of the others closer to my age are married, making this a good assignment for them if they want or have kids. I haven't met a couple of the guys face to face. And don't forget, two are women. I know both of them personally but haven't actually worked with either of them."

"There are women SEALs?"

"No, not all of these people are SEALs. They aren't all Navy. In fact, only my support staff and one team member is. They are all elite forces for one thing or another."

"Oh, but if they're all powerhouses like you, I'm not sure I can handle that. Too much testosterone in one small area could start an explosion."

"They take charge when necessary, yes, but they all answer to me. Each member has specific skills we need to make a diverse team. It's like building your SEAL teams, all areas are necessary, but sometimes you only need a few to complete a mission or task. Otherwise, they're normal people with fairly normal lives. This is a plum assignment for those who need the change. They're here to see if they are a fit with each other and the overall mission."

"Like you."

He kissed her. "No, I fit. I'm the standard they have to meet. When they get here, I'll formally introduce each one of them. That should help."

Alli wondered out loud, how many would show up, Zayden laughed. "All of them."

"What? How do you know?"

"Listen, sweetheart, when I invite my team to show up to a barbeque, they show up."

She nodded sagely. "Oh, it was *that* kind of invitation." He laughed. "And they're new here too. So, it makes the connections and eases the new assignment anxieties. If they meet me in a more casual environment, it helps. It was a great idea to invite your friends." He kissed her again.

The yard was full of military and locals. Zed's newly formed basic team would have six to twelve instructors. He had ten to start, knowing that he would lose a few and gain a few for one reason or another. The remainder in the yard included fire, search and rescue, police, troopers, and then assorted important members of the community that others invited.

"Alli, this is the team as we know them. We'll start with nicknames today and go from there as you become more familiar with military life. These are their 'handles,' so to speak. We operate under the same command as the tier one groups with a different mission. The Joint Special Operations Command or the SOG."

Alli nodded. "Oh, I think I saw that in a documentary. That's like the Raiders, Rangers, and SEALs, and those kinds of groups."

"All the elite groups, the very elite, fall under this command, and as we will be training and doing maneuvers with the cream of the crop from inside and outside the military, it worked best this way. Chime in when I call your name. Brick, Sneakers, Charm, Savi, Mist, Johnny, Cowboy, Chute and the beauties of the group, Catcher and Star. You'll get more later, but for now, work on those names. I know you don't all know each other, but that's what today marks. The beginning. As of today, you are a team. Learn each other, start to identify each other's strengths and weaknesses. I'm obviously Commander Zayden "Zed" Wellesley, and this is my lovely lady, Alesha."

He introduced her to his support staff, and she couldn't remember all of their names. One was Gage as in shotgun. The woman was Martel or Mardell or something. Then there was a kid, really, whose name started with an 'S' and finally, Zed's aide was a man she couldn't recall his name because his presence distracted her from all else. He looked like he ate nails for snacks. Alli decided to stay clear of him, but his wife was very sweet. Odd match.

While the team was nice, they were speaking a different language full of acronyms. With the addition of the other members of the scientific research and testing teams invited as well, Alli decided to do a little cramming on terminology soon. The language was rather abrasive at times. She was glad the children had been corralled away from most of the chatter.

She walked into the kitchen to begin bringing the side dishes out under the industrial awning that Zed had ordered for the many iffy days, like today, when he wanted to do things outside. Zed walked past Alesha as he grabbed the meat to start cooking and seeing no one else was around, he set the platter on the counter, backed her into the wall and kissed her, running his tongue along the seam of her lips before she opened. He deepened the kiss.

Zed's warm breath drifted over her cheek as he spoke with confidence. "Tonight, after the kids are asleep, I'm going to strip you bare, kiss every inch of you, and teach you how I celebrate the fourth. My fireworks will be so much more satisfying than the ones you'll see later."

"Is that right?"

"Mmm-hmm." The kids were squealing loudly as they rounded the corner to the kitchen. Alli giggled when Zed groaned. "I forgot that children interrupt their grownups at the most inopportune times."

"Hush, they're going to my house right now."

"Look, daddy, we're having a parade. Hey, were you kissing my Alli?" asked Kami.

"Yes, I was."

"Oh, okay, but you have to wait so you can watch our parade. Just like the one we saw in town. Could Uncle Chopper fly his helicopter with the flag for us?"

Without waiting for an answer, she led the other younger children in a vigorous march out the door for a further performance in the yard. Zed followed them outside with the platter of raw meat in hand, and Alli directed the two college-age girls to lead the parade and the rest of the children in attendance to her house.

Alli had never hosted this large a gathering, and when the fireworks arrived in full military complement, she was tired. She'd smiled until her face hurt. She'd educated people on the area, discussed everything from winter sports to surviving the rain and snow. Zed had also snagged her to make rounds so he could introduce her when he introduced himself to their guests. Alli couldn't recall half the names. Her friends seemed to enjoy it all.

By the time the evening's fireworks were over, the children had fallen asleep, and Alli's brain was fried along with the remnants of fireworks paper. Calling out their good night as the final guests left, soon they had the last plate sitting in the sink and the last door locked. "I'm so tired I could sleep for a week."

"Tomorrow is my last day off duty. I need to go over the schedule with you as you have the first day with the kids."

"Schedule, really? It's summer, Zed."

He kissed her lips and steered her toward his bedroom on the opposite side of the house from the children's bedrooms. He loved the separation. The baby monitor in the twin's room worked well. "You sound like the children. You're tired. After you get some sleep, you won't be so grumpy."

"I'm tired, not grumpy. I'm also an adult who deals with elementary age children all the time. I don't need a schedule. We will find loads to do."

"Nonetheless, we'll discuss it tomorrow."

When Zayden took on that tone, Alli stopped arguing. She wasn't engaging in verbal warfare.

"Fine."

Zed hated when she gave in with "fine." She knew he would talk, and she would listen and then do as she thought best. And so did he.

"Good, now what about that late-night snack you promised me?"

"Mmm, just follow me, sir, I have plenty for you to snack on."

"Alli, you know I want you here for good." He leaned down for a slow, teasing kiss.

After a kiss like he just gave her, pulling herself out of the fog was difficult.

"Nice foreplay, frogman, but I'm just next door. I love my house."

"Frogman, huh? Commander to you, woman." He nuzzled her neck and nipped it then soothed the offense with his tongue. "Keep it, rent it out, whatever you want to do, but I want you in my bed every night."

"Zed, we are together most nights." She moaned as he released one breast for the other, the cool air puckering her nip painfully. It sent another zing to her sex.

"Alli, honey, I mean come home here, not sneak in after ten."

"I'm not sneaking." She wiggled as he descended down her belly with his magic tongue and lips. Her breath became labored.

"Good then move in," Zed said.

His lips had landed on her clit, and Alli made her delicious noises. Zed's moan meshed with hers.

"Stop wiggling." He slapped her thigh with just enough sting to make the familiar tingle in her deepest places ramp up, and the release of arousal cream, copious. The man lapped it up, curling his tongue around her clit.

"Not fair, Zayden."

"All's fair in love and war, baby. I play to win. You know that." He went in for the kill.

THE NEXT MORNING, ZAYDEN entered the kitchen, right into an epic fight he was sure they were both spoiling for, and each regretted the moment it ended. Zed knew all about transitions, his whole life seemed to be adjusting for them. It could be hell on relations until you worked as a cohesive unit. They weren't there yet, and as he shifted his focus the last week to the job site, he'd dropped the ball at home. While hindsight always identified the problem, it usually came too late to avoid the small detonations.

"Morning baby. I'm doing PT, then we can talk about the schedule."

"I'm awfully busy today, so could we just skip the unnecessary schedule and let me handle them. Write one up for when you have Samantha on day two. I've got my days covered."

"I know you have a lot going on, which is why a schedule will keep everyone on time and focused." Zed walked into the study and brought back two pages.

Alli glanced at it while she sat out cereal and bowls for the children when they got up. Something she'd started to do each morning after she spent the night so she could direct them to a better breakfast choice. She sat out fruit. Zed could do his run now instead of prepping the breakfast himself. He didn't seem to bat an eye that she'd taken over that little task.

"You've got to be kidding. I'm doing double duty these last two weeks, working on the children's festival and trying to help you keep up with things here along with my own obligations besides the festival, and you want me to follow this? No, absolutely not."

"Alli, these are my children, and I have to know they are not wasting their days."

"Zayden, that *is* the definition of children in summer. Look, I have to go. When I have them, I will control their days. When you have them, or someone else does, then you can direct all you want."

Zed remembered a disagreement with Chrissy after the twins were born. Chrissy had backed down. That was not going to happen this time. The militant look that Alesha was displaying told him that very clearly.

Alli slammed out the door, and Kade appeared in the kitchen a few moments later. So much for the run. Zed would have to work on other equipment today. He had a lot on his plate as well. He thrived on the pressure. Alli obviously didn't.

Late that afternoon, Alli returned home and called Zed.

"Zed, I'm sorry about this morning. Things got out of hand."

"Truce?"

"Truce," she agreed with a sigh.

"Thank God. Look, I don't think I was wrong, but I can agree that so long as you don't do anything unsafe, it's up to you how you spend the day."

Alli laughed. "Good thing because I was going to do it anyway."

"I was afraid of that. I probably should address your obstinance, but I like it, and I have more pressing needs."

"Oh? What is that Commander?"

"I need you in my bed tonight."

"Good because I need in your bed tonight, too."

AS THEY TRIED TO GET a new routine to work, both at home and away from home, some days, they accomplished the goal better than others. Zed's job was invigorating and stressful at the same time as he grappled with putting the training program together. The resistance he hadn't expected from some of those assigned to the research and testing components added a layer of bullshit. Zed handled it and was fairly certain he'd made his needs and thoughts clear. It helped that he had the full backing of a large spread of entities.

Homeland security was becoming more than just a handler of domestic border patrol issues. Those were huge but add to it, airdropped drugs and the growing production in the country, human trafficking, their expertise had to be varied. Then they always protected the waterways violations, even pirating, from people who thought the rules were for others, not them.

It didn't help that the politicians who were supposed to look out for the country spent more time than profitable battling among themselves. Zed didn't want on that soapbox any more than he wanted to delve into base territorial prostrating. But he could train men and women to respond in defense of this country and its citizens and do a damn good job of it.

Finally, it seemed as though he'd settled the land around him, the children were in a happy place, his routine at home and in the training center was becoming established, and for the first time since he was handed this position, he could see things take shape. Alli's classes would start back again, and the children would start school soon. With everything, a whole new round of transitions and adjustments would need to happen. Alli was still resisting the move. It was time she joined the family. He knew he'd have to be patient. Some days, patience was in short supply.

For the first time in several weeks, he didn't come home grumpy. Zed hated being out of sorts now that he was comfortable with Alli in every part of his life. He dropped his guard with her, sometimes taking out his work frustrations on her and the kids. He was still finding it hard to relax on his strict safety rules when Alli had the children, so when he found the four of them laughing and playing on the dock while waiting for him, his calm mood shifted.

"What are you doing here?" He did not deliver his words kindly.

Alli looked puzzled. "I have a meeting, so we thought we would wait for you. We could make the switch off faster."

He nodded to the kids. "They're playing too close to the water without life preservers. They could drown. The twins don't swim well, and the water is too cold, anyway."

"There's nothing wrong with them being here, Zed. Besides, I'm a strong swimmer should one of them decide to take a jump."

"The water is too cold to do well. At this temperature, the survival rate drops–"

"Believe me, if I thought that falling in was even a consideration, I would invoke your name to quell any playful childhood antics."

"You hope."

"No, you hope. I can guarantee it would kill the joy out of any activity. You've got to stop acting like the Gestapo and get over yourself, Commander. These children will grow up happy, healthy, and safety-wise if you don't shove it down their throats. Otherwise..."

"Otherwise?"

"You'll take their childhood away by demanding they be little commanders in training. I'm going now."

"Alesha."

His low toned word spoke volumes. Chills chase tremors up Alli's spine as she contemplated his use of that heavy warning voice interspersed with gravel he often used to get her attention. She bit her lip. Having this conversation in a whole different venue with the outcome likely to be different, was, well, irritating and hot. The tingling in her lower belly signaled a release of lubricating arousal. That sensation brought her dangerously close to rubbing her belly and moaning her need. And it pissed her off.

Snap out of it, Alli. This is important. Straightening her stance, she graced him with a hard stare.

"Stop being an overbearing, non-conforming ass, Zayden. No one likes a bully. It demeans us all."

She walked off the dock, on wobbly legs, proud she'd spoken up. It was only after she'd made several attempts with shaky hands to buckle her seat belt, that she looked back at the dock. It was then she noticed how large her audience was. Not only had she forgot the children were there but that the commander rode over with members of his ever-growing training team and support staff along with any other random person who was returning from the smaller island. Damn.

ALLI AND ZADEN'S RELATIONSHIP had been stilted recently, and she hadn't spent the night since she'd stormed off the dock, four days ago. That put them both in a bad mood, and the children were cranky due to the discord they could feel. The festival was last weekend. Zed had taken the children on his own, and while they seemed to have a good time, she was miserable.

Alli started work the next day, and school started in a few days. She had decided to take the children to the beach for a picnic as a last hurrah when Zayden snagged her to discuss his school schedule. It was her last day to be with the children before life changed yet again, and that was the last thing Alli wanted to talk about. Zed spoke of times for pickups, snacks, homework, chores, and other things she tried not to tune out but did. Finally, he'd quit talking.

"Thank you for the run down, I'm sure we will be just fine. Come down to the beach with us, and we can have lunch. I start work tomorrow, and we'll have less opportunity to enjoy the nice days."

Zed hesitated and then said, "You guys go down without me, and I'll be there as soon as I've made up the duty roster and a few other prep things for our meeting tomorrow."

"You won't be long, right?"

"I won't be long."

When Zed strode across the beach behind their houses an hour later, he saw his little family and Alli, whom he missed so much it was a physical ache, enjoying the sand and sea life. Zed knew he loved her, but she needed to learn what life with him was going to be like, and they hadn't had enough time for that. He'd been on vacation and hadn't worked long hours yet, but now life really began tomorrow. They'd both be working.

As Zed waved to the kids, he noticed Kade had a smoking stick that he was swinging around like a sword. Zed would need to have a talk with him because he didn't understand the dangers it posed. Kade swung the stick one more time, hitting the fire pit and knocking large embers into the air. One landed on the top of a red plastic container Zed recognized as the gas for his lawnmower. Running, he grabbed the handle and tipped the container. With his shirt sleeve covering his hand, he knocked the large ember off. It had burned sufficiently into the plastic that it was difficult to remove it.

He looked at his son, who was visibly upset at having his stick taken away and then looked at Alli, who was calmly replacing the last ember back into the fire with a small fireplace shovel. It was her that he focused his attentions on.

"What are you doing, bringing gasoline to the beach?"

"Well, it's been raining off and on, and nothing would have burned."

"Except gasoline, you mean."

"It's an accelerant."

"And dangerous around children."

"I found it in the front yard next to their game balls. How less dangerous was that?"

"It wasn't. I should have moved it, but I didn't take it to the beach and then let them play with fire around it."

"I didn't let him do anything of the sort. He grabbed the stick. I had already told him to put it down. If you had paid attention, you would have seen me on my way to retrieve it."

"It's too little too late. You wouldn't have noticed that there was a large ember burning its way through the container until the big whoosh."

"The likelihood is small that it would have done that. The liquid volume is more likely to have put out the ember assuming it was hot enough for long enough to burn through and fall in."

His voice wavered. "That's more chance than I am willing to take when it could have taken away everything I loved." They were both yelling by now.

That stopped her. Zed was angry but at himself as much as Alli or even Kade. He had fire starter sticks, and he should have covered that with her. He should have done more prep. Dammit, that's why he had a schedule. There were so many more outdoor activities to do here, but that also raised the danger quotient. Maybe he didn't know what he'd agreed to, coming here. His children were his life, and now Alli was in that category, and it scared him to think he could lose them because of a stupid accident. Not again.

"I'll take the children home and then come talk to you in a bit." He was talking to Alli as though she were a naughty child. He didn't see her as one, but right now, he needed to gain control. She seemed confused by his manner. She nodded and began to clean up the lunch items.

"We will get things cleaned up, and the fire put out." Zed began to toss things in the bag Alli had retrieved them from.

Without another word, she walked in the direction of her house, and Zayden called a babysitter. Today, he'd hurt her feelings and made her angry, but this was a safety issue, and he would never bend on those. As he calmed down, he began to realize just how over the top he had gotten after Chrissy was gone. Alli was right. The children would not grow healthily if he stifled the natural learning that growing up should be. He would have to find a way to bring his fears under some kind of control.

After getting the children in front of an unscheduled movie, something he would like to point out to Alli but wouldn't be able to, he closed the door and picked up the phone. He hit Alli's programmed number, and it went straight to voice mail.

He opened the door to the kids and said, "I'm running over to Alli's house."

"She's not home, daddy."

"What?"

"She was driving her car when we were coming off the beach."

How the hell did he miss that? What was wrong with him? He usually knew the environment and the dangers, or changes and here he'd left the gasoline out where the kids played, didn't notice her car gone or that she'd driven away. He went back into his office and left a message on her cell phone. He canceled the sitter.

The children were in bed, and he still hadn't heard back from Alesha. He was worried. He called Jenn from the café.

"Hello?"

"Jenn, it's Zayden Wellesley.

"Hey, how are you."

"Not as good as I'd like. Say, is Alesha there?"

"She was, but she left a couple of hours ago."

Zed used his parental command voice, "Are you positive?"

"Absolutely. Boy, Alli said you could turn on the commander's voice at the drop of a hat. Anyway, she was pretty mad at you and then herself. Finally, by the time she left, I think she was worried that you and she were over. And she might have gone with Craig to get a drink."

"And he went with her?" Ballsy fucker. "Well, we aren't over, so if you see her again, you let her know that and to get her ass home. Tell her I'm looking for her and to check her messages."

"I will. Are you okay? I mean, you sound scary."

"I'm fine." Zed calmed down. "I'm just a jerk, and we had words." He chuckled. "She's good at those."

"Words? Yeah, she can be. Zed, she'll be fine. She knows this island, so she'll be safe. She's the most cautious person I know."

"Unless Craig isn't a gentleman, or she had one too many drinks, drives after drinking or any number of other scenarios."

"You do like to make sure the picture has all the details, don't you? Okay, I'll call around."

All Jenn got in return was a dissatisfied grunt before he hung up. Jenn called Alli. She answered.

"Call your man and check your messages, girl."

"I'm having a good time with my wine glass and visiting. Craig is still awful, even after a few drinks." Alli noted dryly.

"Listen, that man is going to find you, and I don't hold high expectations for your mood or survival rate when he does."

"No, he won't. He thinks I'm an unsafe person. Safety above all things for Commander Wellesley."

"He's crazy about you. I wish a man would look at me with that type of adoring expression on his face, but girl, you are so right about the 'Me Tarzan You Jane,' thing. I think he tried to turn it on with me to get me to tell him what he wanted to know. And I don't know about your dynamics, but if I was in the wrong, I'd be worried he'd show up all John Wayne style, looking for a fireplace shovel."

Alli's voice was panicked. "Oh, God, he didn't have one, did he?"

"What? No, we spoke on the phone. Alli, what are you not telling me?"

"Nothing, it was the John Wayne statement and the wine talking. Thanks, Jenn. You're a good friend."

I hope you think so after I send this message. Jenn pressed the green send button. "She's fine. She's enjoying the hotel bar. You know the one. I think she's worried about what a confrontation will look like when she finally gets home."

"I think she knows exactly what it will look like. Thanks."

Zed had called Samantha back after his conversation with Jenn. She'd just arrived. Zed was thankful for Friday nights, and college kids who needed cash. Zed threw a few items in his pack and went over to his woman's house while trying to decide how he'd accomplish what he needed to do.

Jumping in his SUV, he arrived at the hotel he'd stayed at on his recon trip. His resolve strengthened as he remembered the incredible sex they'd had here. He didn't see her car in the parking lot, so he scoured the bar with no luck. Craig was there looking three sheets to the wind with nothing coherent to say when Zayden approached him. *Not worth the effort.* The bartender said Alli was headed to get gas and go home.

"If you're Zayden, then Alli is not happy with you, but by the time she left to go home, she no longer added curse words to your name. She is in deep with you, man. Go get her and take care of her. She's a good person."

"She drove off after drinking?"

"Not while I was here. She was already here, and I did see a wine glass when I came on. I don't know what number it was, but I only served her a soft drink. She left, walking straight and sounding fine."

"Roger that."

Chapter Fourteen

Alli pulled into the driveway and turned off the car. She looked over at Zayden's semi-dark house and felt the tears form a puddle again. Why had she taken off like that? Jenn said he assured her he was not breaking up, but it was obvious he didn't care enough to find her and bring her home. It was, however, enough to fuel her beverage choice. Well, it did, except she wasn't a drinker, and the moment she'd felt the effects of her third wine, she stopped and switched to water and pop. Yeah, no drinking problems, just man troubles and that, tonight, was so much worse.

She'd finally come home when someone she didn't know came onto her, hard. She almost called Zayden but decided to just leave. Alli stood up to go, unaware another guy was leaning over her. His drink went all over her, and it wasn't a little wine. Reeking, the bartender took pity and tossed her a t-shirt from the last contest that said, "Winning Tits." It was definitely time to go home.

His intention was to take a shower and go to bed. No calls from Zed. No angry man at her doorstep, no concerned lover looking for her. Glancing at the display on her phone, she saw it was midnight. Zed was leaving at seven to make his boat and his first official day of training for his team. He'd worked practically nonstop, and his people loved him. She loved him too, but it appeared to be one-sided. Alli had planned to break through their wall of discord and sleep over there tonight, but that would not happen. She turned the knob, and the door was wrenched open by none other than a very irritated man. Her man.

Stunned, she simply stared. "Um, what are you doing here?"

He ignored her question and shot off another one instead. "Where the hell have you been?"

Stunned at first, Alli giggled. Zayden sniffed the air. "Alesha Campbell, you'd better not be drunk, little girl, because you're in so much trouble now, that you have no idea what being intoxicated would do to your future state of comfort."

That snapped her out of the confusion. "What? No, I'm not drunk, regardless of how I smell. Can you either go home or get out of my way? I need a shower and a bed. You should be in bed too, you have to work tomorrow.

"Take your shower, I'll wait."

"No, you won't wait, and why are you here, anyway? How did you get in? Oops, never mind that one."

"Yes, because you know very well how I got in, how anyone could get in if they had a mind. Something we'll discuss later. I'll get us something to drink."

"Water for me, please."

"Because you have had too much already."

"No, dammit, because I have had too much spilled on me already. God, you're such a sanctimonious ass sometimes. And bossy, dictatorial, and... and highhanded."

Zed snagged her around the waist and yanked her close, kissing her ear that was blushed red and warm. He spoke low.

"Highhanded, huh? I've never been called that before. I kinda like it. I could live up to that title."

She rolled her eyes as he referred to a play on words. She ignored his meaning. "You already do. It means bossy, controlling, self-righteous—"

He spoke with his lips just above hers. "I know what it means, woman, and you haven't seen anything yet." His lips pressed against hers, taking what he wanted, angling his head to get even more. She moaned as his kiss, laced with something akin to desperation, took her breath away. When she lifted for a fresh gulp of air, he pulled her in tighter leaving one hand on her waist, and one hand slid into her hair, securely clenching the tangled strands in his fingers.

"You're right, you aren't drunk. But you're stinky and still in so much trouble. Go take your shower, sweetheart."

He dropped another quick kiss on her lips, nipping her lip before giving her an indulgent little smile. It was hot as hell and just as infuriating, but it meant he wasn't insanely angry. She'd take it. They'd be all right. Alli knew there was still groveling in her future, but he had some too. Zed stepped back and patted her bottom before releasing her to shower.

When she returned, Zayden was all business again.

"Have a seat, we have a little ground to cover." He wasn't smiling now, but, for some reason, it didn't worry her. "Why did you take off? I mean, what was that all about?"

"I know it sounds silly now, but I didn't like being sent home like a naughty child."

He huffed a sound that could have been a laugh. "Taking the plastic gas container to the beach with a fire and children *is* being naughty, but I love that wayward woman. She's cute, generous, and accepting. I should have handled it differently, but when I thought of what I could have lost if the gas container had caught on fire..." He shook his head as though removing the mental picture of his family hurt or worse from his head.

She sucked in a guilty breath. "I should have paid more attention. I love those munchkins and wouldn't let anything happen to them if I could help it. I'm sorry I wasn't watchful enough."

"Oh, baby, I had no worry you would protect them, but it was a careless mistake that could have cost us more than we could afford to pay." He paused. "I could have lost everything that meant anything to me."

The sobering thought brought tears to her eyes. "I know," she whispered. "But you spoke to me like I think you speak to your office staff when you are irritated, as though I was incompetent. I got angry."

"Yes, when I'm worried or stressed, I tend to take on my Commander role. Right or wrong, it's who I am. I guess now is the time you need to decide if life with me, the children, everything that would entail, is what you want. Sweetheart, submission is a dirty word in today's society, but, to an extent, it's what I'm asking. To accept my leadership in the home between us. There can be only one in every relationship. One who has the ultimate say those few times it is necessary. We've been living it already. You have allowed me to decide areas you could have made a choice but stepped back. Are you willing to allow me to take care of you in every way? It isn't just during sex when you like me to be macho, it's about a life built on trust and mutual accountability."

Alli wanted what he described. His tone, his take-charge attitude. She mattered enough to Zed that he took notice of what happened in her life. The thing that stuck with her was she knew she could say 'no' to anything, and he would respect it. She was positive she would push back on some of his edicts in the future, but right now, he flipped her switch like no other man ever did or ever would. But submission? Nope. She struggled with that word. That was not this girl's cup of tea.

She looked into his warm eyes, which seemed to say how much he loved her. It was tangible. It warmed her to her very soul. She believed he really did, and she knew she loved him. He sat, rubbing small circles on her back as he waited for her decision. He gave the impression he had all the time in the world to wait on her.

"Does that mean you want to be the boss of me?" she asked teasingly.

He laughed. "Sometimes. I love you, and I want it to work with every fiber of my being, but this was a big, careless mistake. And then you put yourself in further danger by traipsing off to a bar. Drinking never solved anything, and going with a waste of space like Craig Harlow is enough to bring down retribution. There was nothing safe about that. I'm surprised he went with you."

"Funny you should say that. He was a little nervous when I asked to tag along with him. He said something about pushing his luck."

"Good. No going near Craig Harlow again, agreed?"

"Agreed."

"No taking off when you're irritated because, in that state, you could have an accident. No more using alcohol as a response to heightened emotions. No scaring your man to death anymore, right?"

"Right." She gave him a wry smile. "I know it was risky, but I was careful and really, I wasn't intoxicated or even near the limit. Craig was just available."

A grunt was Zed's only response.

"No more taking off when you are angry or feel hurt. We talk it out. You can take a time out but not time off. Next time I will consider it AWOL and respond accordingly."

She didn't need to ask him how that would manifest itself. She had her suspicions.

"Got it." She looked longingly at him and ran her finger across his chest. "Zayden..." she whimpered.

"I know, sweetheart, I need it too." He reached to pull her leggings and underwear off. "Straddle me." He positioned her over his powerful thighs facing him.

Alli had no problem complying with this request. She slid her legs apart and settled into position. It was a little embarrassing, but she craved his touch more than she felt awkward. Zed lightly tapped her puffy labia, playing with her sensitive bits.

"So wet and ready for me. Such a sexy girl. You know I always ache for you. I don't think my cock has been at ease since I met you."

Going to work rubbing her clit, he placed one rough finger and then two inside her sheath. He brought his arousal coated fingers to her bottom, easing his legs apart enough to open her cheeks wider so he could tease the muscle ring there. Alli had had no one touch her there before Zed, and she couldn't believe how it turned her on. She held as still as she could to encourage more play. When he didn't breach her opening, she groaned her frustration. He patted her hot wet center, and the sting had her suck in air noisily.

"My time, baby."

Alli couldn't believe how amazing the bottom sensations were and how tightly sprung it made her.

"You're awfully greedy for a woman who just barely skirted having her ass addressed for her misbehavior."

He swatted her butt twice, and she made a new round of desperate whimpers.

"Zed, please."

Placing Alli on her feet, Zed stood. He flipped her over the arm of her sofa and scolded, "Don't move."

The fast rasp of his zipper as it raced down its track heightened her awareness. She heard the belt buckle rattle as she took the belt off. Her core twitched, her bottom followed suit.

"What did I say to you?"

"Sorry, sorry, I can't help it."

She heard the leather cut through the air, causing a breeze. "Ahh. Okay, I'm trying."

Warm hands landed on her hips, holding her steady, caressing her ass. Alli wiggled her bottom in her eagerness. He swatted her ass again, leaving a burn that heated her up more.

"You just have to be an imp, don't you? I think it's in your DNA."

"How did you guess?"

He landing an ouchy, stinging stripe down but then tossed his belt to the floor. His hands rubbed the sting and intensified it.

When Zed hesitated, Alli groaned her frustration. "Zayden."

Her desperate attempt at pointing a neon sign over her dark entrance encouraged Zayden to take it. Her cream was scooped up, and her entrance was coated as was his cock. He breached Alli's bottom hole, piercing deep down to her core, his ball bouncing off her ass.

Zed's penetration savagely jolted her. He was careful but persistent. She came hard, screaming and holding her place while he slammed into her ass over and over. She'd no desire for gentle, her arousal was almost animalistic, sucking in his cock as he claimed her hard, rubbing against soft, pliant tissue and bringing her aching body to climax again. He followed with a grunt of satisfaction and release as Alli almost wept again with the strength of her climax. He was like a drug and no longer emerging, she was totally addicted. She knew there would be plenty of trials, but he got her in all her quirky needs, and that was enough for her.

ALLI WAS SPENDING MOST of her time at Zed's. She'd gotten to the point that she had her own routine, and it involved take out dinner on Friday, the one weekday the housekeeper didn't come. Tonight, Alli had picked up dinner, and it was soon devoured. The little ones had two hours practicing with the local children's theater, so the adults were alone. Sitting in the living room, sipping their coffee, Alli snuggled into Zed as he drew her close for a kiss.

"I have to take the team out to train in a week."

"What does that mean exactly?"

"I'll be gone for a couple of weeks. The final logistics were just finished, but I won't have much phone contact. Maybe I should call my mother to come up for that time."

"Zed, I promise we can handle it. So long as you have the proper paperwork in place for emergencies, have the sitters in place when I'm not here, and Kerry doesn't leave on vacation during that time, I don't think it will be any harder than it is now."

"I don't want to put any extra strain on you or the schedule. I won't be here to smooth things over when life gets scrambled. No second driver."

"Sweetheart, you don't do that now. Yes, you're a second driver, but you're so plan oriented we often skip you. You may make huge adjustments on the job, but at home, you're anal-retentive about schedules. We'll do fine."

"If you're sure. I don't seem to run this house any longer, anyway."

"Silly man. You never did, but if it makes you feel any better, I'll take them to my house."

Zayden chuckled. "No, stay here." He dropped a kiss on her nose and gave her a mock-serious look. "Do not make any irreverent changes while I'm gone."

"Irreverent to whom?"

"My way of life and my peace of mind."

Alli made a production of sighing loudly and rolling her eyes. "You aren't a religion, Zayden."

"True, but I like to think I'm the undisputed law."

"If you need that." Her eyes sparkled as she teased him.

"What I need is you, in my bed, letting me have my way with you."

"Ah, now on that, we agree."

"I love you."

"I love you. We have one problem, though."

"What?"

"I'll miss you and the extracurricular things while you're gone."

"Absence is supposed to make the heart grow fonder. I guess I could wear you out this week, so you'll need two weeks to recover, huh?"

"That might work, but don't count on it."

The following Monday, oh dark thirty, Alli kissed Zayden goodbye, and with his final instructions and admonitions ringing in her ears, she let him go.

As the two-week marker came and went, Alli was disappointed when he didn't come home, but Zed had said they might be a day or two later. When day four past his expected return arrived with no Zayden, she called his office. Bolton, Zed's aide, who was never very helpful, was more than eager to accommodate today.

"The commander said to make sure you got what you needed if you called. I'll let you know as soon as I get in contact with them."

Later that afternoon, Bolton called back. "Miss Campbell? "Yes?"

"Bolton here. I've been in contact with the team, and they're operational."

"You will have to be more specific for me. They are well and on their way home?"

"Well, ma'am, yes and no. They will all be home but not right away."

"Explain, please."

Bolton seemed to be searching for words. "Well, ma'am, the commander is um, delayed."

Alli had had enough of the double talk and avoidance. "Damn it, just spit it out, Bolton. If you can't, then get me someone who can. Better yet, get me the commander himself."

Bolton's tone became formalized and efficient. No more pussyfooting around. "Ma'am, the commander has had an accident causing a concussion. He will arrive at the hospital within the hour."

"How severe?"

"Ma'am?"

"How severe is his concussion?"

"No idea, ma'am. He'd lost consciousness."

After bleeding the man for information, agonizing word by agonizing word, she called Samantha to gather the children after school and take them home. She met Zed's team as they arrived at the hospital emergency department. Brick and Savi walked straight to Alli and immediately began to settle her nerves. Brick put his arms around her, pulling her close. These men were so confident, one wouldn't know they were all close to her age.

"Brick, how is he?"

"Cowboy says he had a good-sized hit, so the concussion is significant enough, but he'll be fine if there isn't much swelling and no bleeds. It's a good thing the Commander has a hard head. Not as hard as mine, but sturdy enough."

"Brain swelling?"

Savi nodded. "Cowboy figures there is at least some swelling. We had a small landslide which we circumvented fine, but an unstable ledge gave way on the last man, that was Zed."

"Mrs. Wellesley?"

"Alli," prompted Cowboy, "the doctor needs to speak with you."

The look he gave her said to play along. She did. "Yes? Will he be alright?"

The physician knew her but only as a nurse who used to pull shifts in the ER as a backup. He wouldn't know if she had married or not.

"We have testing to do, but I have every confidence he will be fine. You can see him for a minute while we get the scans ready."

Alli asked the Doctor a few appropriate questions and then followed the nurse to Zayden's room. She was led into the room while every man and woman on his team except Brick, headed for the waiting room. Seeing Zed laying on a gurney bed, rails up, IV's in, no movement, and face grease still on in places, she had to check that it was him.

She moved blankets and clothing away, burrowing down to his chest, where she knew there was a small brown oval birthmark, similar to a thumbprint. Nothing spectacular, but he insisted Alli know he had demanded she know it existed in case she had to identify his body. She had balked at the conversation at the time, but now, she was so thankful he was persistent.

Scanning his broad, beautiful chest, Alli spied it. It was the irrational assurance she needed. As she leaned down, Alli kissed his pec right over the mark. The skin was salty and gritty.

Tears filled her eyes. At this very moment, he should be standing in a shower, not laying on this hospital bed.

She pulled away from Zed enough to place her supple lips on his dry ones. He was capable and firm with everyone but his family. With them, he was also their rock, their protector. After this trip, she was sure the team's bond had grown into a deeper level of trust. Zed said they would grow stronger as their connection grew.

She vowed to get to know the rest of these people who, instead of dropping him at the hospital and going home to clean up, getting some well-deserved downtime, had settled in for the long haul, acting as though there was nothing else they wanted to do. They might not all stay with the training site, but it didn't matter, they all took care of one of theirs. Today that was Zayden. That made them special to her.

Alli sat in the waiting room while Zed had scans and was moved to his room. They didn't place him in ICU since he showed only a slight brain swelling due to the trauma. Nothing else seemed to have been affected. No brain bleeds. As soon as they got the swelling down, then all else would be well. The group took up a vigil by twos. Alli insisted they all go home, but since they rejected that idea, they compromised on shifts. By the time Sneakers and Johnny had returned, Zed had just woken up.

"Alli, baby." In his weakened state, his voice sounded subdued, but she heard him.

"Hey. Don't talk. Just get better. I've got everything at home under control, and the team has all the rest covered."

"Go home, Alli."

"When I can take you with me."

"No, go now." Sneakers, always so quiet, spoke from behind Alli.

"Hey, sir. Looking slightly better. You shouldn't talk right now. Alli is right. Everything's good."

"I want her out of here. Take her home. That's an order."

The effort to speak was more than Zed could do. He fell back to sleep. Sneakers led her out so she could cry. Johnny was already calling in the troops. Cowboy and Catcher walked in behind Johnny. Cowboy walked right up to Alli and gave her a hug before handing her a sandwich from the Coffee Cache.

"You need to pull yourself together here, girl. I'm not one for sugar-coating things, so here it is. Zed is vulnerable in his weakened state. Not something he wants you to see. That man adores you, and there isn't a person on Quartz island or this island that would tell you differently. He loves you, but you need to give him space. Pride is a terrible thing, but for men and women like us, it's deep-seated. In our line of work, perception can be everything, and he wants to maintain that persona of control."

Tansy "Catcher," sat next to Alli and shoulder bumped her. "Men are asses. They all are. Some you can live with anyway, and some you give the boot. I'd give the commander the boot, myself. As a C.O., he rocks most of the time, but as a man, I wouldn't think he'd be very passionate. I mean, he's a cold son of a bitch."

"I don't know who you know, but my Zed is kind, loving, protective. He wouldn't let anything hurt us or cause us pain."

"Ah, so that's why he keeps kicking you out. He has a misplaced idea you can't handle his injury. I mean, it isn't bad as injuries go, but if you can't handle this, and something bigger happens," Catcher shrugged. "Good to know in advance. He doesn't want to shake the boat."

"That isn't it. Zed is trying to protect me."

"You might be right."

Alli gave the woman an amused grin. "Tansy, you're a good friend. A bit of a bitch, but a good friend."

Tansy shrugged and walked off sporting a brief smile.

"You all are. But if Zed cares, he has to know that I will see his vulnerabilities sometime."

"Not if he can help it," said Brick. "So, let's make it so he can't help it."

Alli refused Zed every time he tried to guilt her to go home. The team rotated between the hospital, running children to school and back, even sleeping at the house with them. It thrilled Samantha to be working so much. Kerry covered dinner.

On day two, when Zed woke up again, Alli was in the cafeteria. Zed was still weak and grumpy.

"Brick, take her home. You all go home. I'm fine. Appreciate the vigil, but it's unnecessary."

"Roger that sir, but if I might take some liberties here, we all think you need to hear a few home truths. That woman out there, she's a keeper. Wife material, if I may say so, sir. I'd be first in line to take her off your hands if that's what you're trying to do, get rid of her." Brick nodded and grinned when Zed's response was a deep growl. "That's what I thought. But that's exactly what you're communicating when you push her away."

Cowboy stepped in. "We all get you not wanting her to see you vulnerable. But sir, if you mess this up, reject her caring for you like your woman should do, there is no fixing it."

Savi nodded. "I believe this is what one would call your Waterloo, sir. How do you want to handle this?"

Zed seemed thoughtful but still refused Alli to come in when he was awake. Alli sat in the room when he slept, took her breaks when he was awake, sitting outside his door or in the waiting room. She wondered if he really was just that damn stubborn or if his feelings didn't run deep enough to share this time with her.

Zed was discharged. He'd spent three days in the hospital, and that was three days too long. His friends didn't change his mind about allowing Alli in. She was a stubborn woman, but he would not scare her into thinking this is what it will be like living with him. He must have changed her mind because she wasn't outside the door when he walked out. He was disappointed. She'd finally done what he asked her to do, and now he regretted that she'd listened. No telling if that ended their relationship or not. Probably did.

When he walked past the waiting room, he was already giving himself another pep talk about this being for the best. Just out of random curiosity, he glanced into the waiting room and there Alesha was, his stubborn woman, sitting, sniffling, sucking on a candy bar.

"Alli."

The woman he couldn't get enough of and who, by all rights, should have kicked his ass to the curb long ago, met his gaze with a deep longing. She sat, sucking food she shouldn't have, but if his team was right, vending machine fare was most of what she'd had despite their efforts at getting her something more nourishing. Her sorrow at his rejection was written across her whole body. The snatches of sleep Cowboy had demanded she take, didn't alleviate the dark shadows below her eyes. An unhealthy pallor replaced the typical rosiness of her cheeks. Her hair limp and messy. What a complete ass he'd been to the woman he loved.

He held out his arms, and instead of ignoring him or yelling at him, telling him he was no longer the love of her life, she sat down the mutilated candy, unfurled her legs from under her bottom and silently stood. As she approached him, her eyes never left his face. Alli was one to show all her emotions, but today, nothing passed over her countenance. He stood there, arms out, entreating her to come to him. She never slowed but walked right into his arms.

"Oh, sweetheart, I'm so damn sorry. I fucked up when I discovered you were waiting for me to regain consciousness. You once accused me of demeaning us, I did that purposely this time, and I was wrong. I hurt you. I don't know how to fix this, Alli, but I love you. Anything you want, it's yours if you promise not to leave me."

"I wondered if I should clear out my things at your house."

"Did I say I was an ass? I love you and thought I would scare you off if you saw me weak."

"I know, Brick and Cowboy said the same thing. Even Catcher tried to set me straight. I love you, and I knew you loved me, but your thinking was wrong. It doesn't make you less of a man if I see you're vulnerable. You're just more precious to me. I would not leave you no matter what you said or did. You needed me there even if you refused to acknowledge it."

Zed leaned down, pressing his lips to hers in a tender kiss. "I missed you. Do you forgive me?"

"Mmm, I missed you. There is nothing to forgive so long as you know the next time you think you can shut me out for whatever reason you contrive in your head, I will bring my hedge clippers with me." The men burst out laughing.

"Received loud and clear, ma'am." His arm slid down to around her waist and pulled her close. "Let's go home, sweetheart."

As the couple said goodbye to the two at the hospital, they promised to call the rest of the team and give them a status. Zed said he would touch base tomorrow. "But tonight is all about my family."

As they were pulling into the cul-de-sac, Alli driving for she refused to get in the car with him at the wheel, Zed spoke, his voice clear and decisive.

"You need a good spanking for disobeying a direct order. An order, might I add, made multiple times."

"I might surmise you need one for trying to dismiss your most important ally. Besides, you can't order me around. I'm not one of your subordinates."

He laughed. "Too bad, this would be so much easier if you were." He nodded. "Point taken."

Zed called his parents later while Alli prepared dinner as it was Friday night, and she wanted real food. The children needed the security of them all sitting at the table, and Zed needed it all. The children spoke to their grandparents. It was as though the whole house sighed in relief. Things were back as they should be.

That night, as he pulled Alli close to him, Zed spoke. "I know that I did things badly this week. And sometimes you think I'm highhanded, or inflexible, which I can be, but we are good together, aren't we? The children adore you. I adore you, and after this week, my team thinks you're untouchable and amazing. In fact, Brick told me if I had no intention of keeping you, he was first in line to receive you. I was too woozy to shoot him, but I wanted to even though he was right to push me."

"Yes, we get things wrong sometimes, but I really think we're good together."

"Alli, I didn't know if I would ever find a woman I could love and who could love those three curtain climbers in there and me, but I did. One who puts up with my demanding ways and injects sanity when I get too controlling at home and lose sight of the real goal, our happiness."

He pulled her even closer and kissed her gently. "My parents tell me I'm no son of theirs if I don't put a ring on your finger. They wanted to thank you again for keeping them updated while I was in the hospital. The children told me they found their new mommy, and I had to stop interviewing you. The guys gave me a talking to, which I have already alluded to, and when my friend Ryder Mason called to check on me, he said I needed to get my head out of my ass and marry you.

To quote him, 'that girl is a good SEAL's wife, and a better commander's partner because if all typical avenues say, *no*, she finds a way to take care of business her way.' I cleaned up the language for politeness." They both laughed.

"I haven't ever met him."

"But I've talked to him about you." Zed grew serious again. "I know three kids is a lot to put on you, and I would want us to have children if you wanted them, but—"

"But we will manage."

"I don't know, maybe I need to rethink this. I don't know if I can keep up with the training center, my men, my kids, and you.

"Wait," she said. "It's getting close to winter, and there is hunting, carving, beading and more language class. And holidays, birthdays..." Alli laughed.

"Plus, soccer, basketball and baseball? Not possible," said Zed.

"Yes, we will have to pick and choose based on aptitude, but not football because of the head injury stats. Then if we have another baby, the world will change yet again."

"I'll need a bigger house."

She laughed. "Yes, probably."

"You're going to be trouble, aren't you, sweetheart?"

"Oh, yeah. But my big bad SEAL can handle it." She reached up to caress his cheek. "Now, about that word obey. It's archaic."

"I agree. I think, *submit* is a much better word."

"Well, maybe it's safer not to mess with tradition."

"If you insist," he agreed as he swooped down for a soul-seeking kiss. Alli might not like the word *obey* or *submit*, but she was more than happy to submit to Zayden's loving.

Chapter Fifteen

L ife had resettled into a comfortable routine after Zed's royal screw up after his concussion. He'd worked hard to normalize their days together, including coming home on time. The reality was, while he was working to build his training program and supervise the assembly of the site, he had often arrived home after the children were in bed. Even then, both he and Alli had work to do, effectively ending their summertime habit of spending every evening together. Zed had offered to share his ample office, but Alli wanted him to have his space. She continued to keep her office work at her house.

Alli had moved much of her seasonal clothing and toiletries over to Zed's room, meaning all of her day to day items, and she'd taken over the running of the house when he wasn't there. Zed still complained about her lack of organization, but no one suffered. With the responsibilities of his work and hers and the children's needs, their relationship felt strained, almost forced at times. The weekends were spent on walks, beachcombing, short hikes, and catch up chores but usually with only one adult in attendance at a time. Things came to a head when Alli offered to take the kids out for an afternoon.

Zed vetoed the idea. "They aren't going without me."

"I've been boating my whole life. I have a Coast Guard certified boat, plenty of gear, and I have taken the small craft mariners' class."

"Good to know, but unless you're going with another adult, you aren't going either. It isn't safe."

"That's ridiculous. I'm probably safer in these waters than you would be, but if that's an issue, come with us."

"I'd love to, but right now I'm swamped with work. It won't always be like this, but for now..." Zed shrugged.

"Are you telling me that you would deny those children because you can't go and don't trust me?"

"Not a trust issue, a safety issue. I told you, you aren't going alone either."

"The hell I'm not."

The kitchen door slammed hard seconds after she stormed out of the study. If he wasn't waiting for a video conference to start, he would have gone after her. Zed knew there would be bridges he would have to mend, and it would probably involve groveling, even after he explained himself better, but at least his family would be safe. Then he heard the engine on her boat start and slammed his fist on the table. He picked up the phone to call her, and it went to voice mail. That woman was in more hot water than she had any idea. She'd find out just how much when he got his hands on her ass. It might even be a paddling offense. His blood was boiling.

Katrina ran into the study. "Daddy, Alli's leaving without us."

"I told her it wasn't safe alone with you three. I guess she went anyway."

"But, Alli said you should never go alone."

"Yes, well, I think she is angry with daddy."

"And now you're mad at her."

"Not mad, disappointed."

"Oh, no. Daddy, you have to promise not to ... um... get mad at her. You'll scare her off, and we haven't married her yet."

"I want to talk to you about what you think daddy does. Now," the video conference rang. "Great. Today they're on time. Okay, daddy has a meeting. Don't worry about Alli, she is not mad. She just needs a break. Things will be fine. Play with the twins, will you?"

"Promise?"

"Promise." As Katrina walked out of the study, Zed prayed he hadn't just lied to his daughter. He turned his attention to his conference call. "Good afternoon, gentlemen."

It had been two days since Alli slammed out of the kitchen, and he'd had enough. She hadn't slept in their bed nor even visited the children, and he was at the end of his rope. Zed was at her door when she came home from classes on the third day.

"We need to talk."

"I'm busy."

"Too bad. We're talking."

"Zed, shouldn't you be at work?"

"I am exactly where I should be, straightening out this mess."

"I don't have anything to say to you."

He followed her into the house. "No problem. I'll talk, you listen."

"Why? You've made it clear my opinion means nothing to you."

"Alesha Campbell, enough. This is childish."

She rolled her eyes at him then tossed her keys, missing the bowl that typically held them and jingling as they hit the tile at her feet. She shoved the table out of the way peevishly, bending down to snatch the keyring off the floor.

"Fine," she said. You can talk but, ow, Zed! Ow! You might swat me in the bedroom, but you aren't doing it in my living room. Ow, that stings."

"I'm happy to discuss everything, but you're listening, remember?"

She ignored his words. "And to put you on notice, there isn't going to be anymore sharing of a bedroom."

She made a production of closing her mouth, crossing her arms before sitting down petulantly and crossing her legs in obstinate attendance. Zed nodded when what he wanted to do was spank her ass red before making hot, nasty, love to her and listen to her climax over and over.

"We need to do something different. I know you think I don't trust you with the kids, but I wouldn't let anyone take them on the water without me in the beginning. I don't think you should go without another adult with you, either. If I ever see you taking off alone like last weekend, you're going to find sitting in your instructor's chair more challenging."

"We don't sit as much in nursing. It's a hands-on job."

"And feeling cocky enough to smart off. It will make it so much easier to follow through. This conversation can turn into a hands-on event as well if you like."

"You don't have the right to..."

"Maybe not now, but I want to have that right. I love you, dammit, and I thought we had gone over all this and agreed, but here it is again. I want you to move in with me permanent-ly."

"But what about the kids, my house..."

He raised his hand. "The kids love you and would be ecsta-tic. They are confused about why you aren't at the house right now. I have an idea about this house. I talked to the powers that be and tossed it out. They like it and are getting the permissions together. They were going to find a place to purchase on the is-land and had me looking. I'd put the realtor on notice. They need to house up to ten trainees as overflow from the center. This place, with some upgrades, would be perfect."

"You did that without consulting with me?"

"Well, I had to find out if it was a viable option before bringing it up with you. It's not like I offered your home, I just found out if it was doable."

"Without asking me." It was a statement. "You don't have that right, Zayden. Get out right now, get out. Just go away."

"What is wrong with you? I only inquired about the feasi-bility. They don't know anything about you having a house."

"Behind my back."

"Not behind your back, in my mind. I do have a few thoughts without you, sweetheart."

She continued as though he'd not spoken. "You don't let me take the children boating, but you can go behind my back and..."

Before she could utter another word, Zed had his lips on hers, his body pressing her into the sofa, kissing her breathless. "I love you, dammit. I might have overstepped the boundaries that you have erected, but I love you. I want you in my bed and messing up my bathroom. I want you to call to find out when

I'm coming home for dinner and chewing me out when I'm late. You've overtaken my heart. I need you in every part of my life."

"What are you saying exactly?"

"Hell, what have I been saying all these weeks, woman?"

"A girl wants to have it laid out for her, Zed."

"She does, huh? Sweetheart, I've asked you to marry me. I told you I love you. But if you need me to say it every day, that is no problem. I love you. I love every incredible, unreasonable, mouthy, disobedient part of you."

"But you didn't. You said others told you to marry me. You said how things would be if we married. But you never actually asked me."

Zed stared at Alli. "I love your laugh, your cry, your moan when I sink deep into your inner sanctum. Like I'm going to do right now. Marry me?"

"Are you sure?"

"The answer is yes, baby, in case you weren't sure. You need to say it so I can make love to you. Then after I make hot, messy, loud, sexy love to you, you can grab your work bag, cause you're moving in."

"Yes."

He kissed her hard as he pushed roughly inside her shirt to unsnap her bra. "Sorry," he said, his voice raspy with desire. "But I need you now. This has to be down and dirty because the kids are coming home in thirty minutes from soccer practice."

He pulled her tee over her head as she unbuckled his belt. She started on his uniform pants. "Can't you get zippers in these?" she mumbled as she struggled with the buttons behind the front flaps.

"Nope, don't want them." He kissed her neck as he allowed her to continue working on the pants.

"Well, I do. They would be easier," she grumbled as Zed laughed and helped her by stepping out of the pants.

His jacket and tee were off quickly, and he had her stripped with little effort. The urgent grunting changed to moans as they took off the edge of their desperation, and the frantic movements had subsided in their urgency. But even though he'd said down and dirty, Zed changed his kisses to less violent plundering, and his touch was tender as he caressed her breasts, taking the puckered nipples into his mouth. Alli often liked things rough, but he wanted to communicate his love was not all wild, barbaric passion. It was solid. He loved her fiercely, and that didn't always take on the savagery he'd started this session with.

He kissed below her ear, and she panted. "You know I came over here to smack your ass for being so careless with your safety and running away from home."

She turned her head to kiss him. "It's a draw."

"You think so? Well, we'll talk about punishment later. I don't think smacking your butt is an effective deterrent. You like it too much. Now, I think we have established withholding orgasms might work better."

She didn't answer, but Zed felt her grab his cock and thumb the sensitive underside. God, she had magic fingers. With just the right amount of pressure, she moved up and down his shaft, moving the foreskin up and down with her hand. The heat built and the telltale tingling that accompanied his efforts to hold out longer grew as the pressure increased.

"Baby, I can't last much longer. You have to stop."

Zed slid her hand off of him and rearranged her to perch on his cock, slowly guiding her to sink on his hard, thick staff. He placed his hands on her hips and prayed she could orgasm without direct clit stimulation because he couldn't get there right now. He shifted to help with the pressure on her nerve center.

All thought ceased except the instinctive mating dance. Zed pumped, and Alli met his movements. The frenzy of earlier returned. "Touch yourself, honey."

She reached down and flicked her own clit. Zed held on to the last vestiges of control as he watched her pleasure herself.

"Alli, that's hot as hell. Finish yourself off." He was gratified to finally hear her orgasming. Her sweet mewls and spasming core muscles shoving him off into his own bliss. When the rushing in his ears receded, he found his woman panting while lying on his chest. They lay silent until his watch signaled his time was up.

"You put an alarm on sex?"

"Had to hon, the kids will be here in five minutes." He began to roll her off his chest. "Gotta get dressed, and you need to pack the rest of your things to bring over."

"Can we talk about this?"

"Yep, at the house. Now move woman, I have to get dressed."

Alli moaned her disappointment. "Tell me it isn't always going to be this way."

"It won't. Sometimes it's worse, but I promise mostly, it will get better." Alli reached for her panties and looked up at a fully dressed man bending to lace his low quarters.

"How do you do that?"

"Dress quickly? Necessity. I'll see you in thirty."

"An hour. I need a shower."

"An hour then. Don't make me come and get you, young lady. You're already in hot water."

"So, what else is new?" She stretched languidly.

He grinned, dropped a kiss on her lips, put his cap on and walked out the door. She went to shower, still wondering what had just happened.

Chapter Sixteen

Alesha brought the children inside and checked the phone for messages but found none. Zayden wanted to complete the full Train the Trainer course with his team before the holidays. He'd been practicing the entire course for months, and the team had been hard at it without a break. Now they were on the last segment, the cold weather hostage snatch-n-go survival exercise. If his scheduling went as planned, Alli expected them to return tomorrow. She had to admit she still had some anxiety after the last time he went out with the team, but Zed assured her it was a freak accident. Alli wasn't sure she believed him, but what could she do. It was the man's job and one he thrived on.

Alli sighed. Would Zayden be okay with her accepting the invitation for a winter hike with the kids? The ground was packed, and the trails had been hiked often enough to be secure. She found she was more nervous about safety when he was gone. More worried about everything, it seemed, which was odd because she had lived her whole life without his over the top safety concerns. Even though it was the middle of winter, the heavy snow had stopped days ago. She needed fresh air. So did the children.

Making her decision, she announced, "Get your winter gear out, guys; we're going for a hike."

The whoops of delight coming from her small charges helped her to push back the ominous feeling of concern. *It's only because my over-cautious caretaker is gone. I guess I need to argue about it before I'm comfortable doing it.* There had been plenty of harshly whispered confrontations in the last months, and it didn't help that Alli was rather free-living, and Commander Wellesley was checklist oriented. Grinning to herself, she went to the kitchen to cook a little breakfast while the kids gathered their packs and dressed.

The morning had stayed clear and bright. The sun was strong, and the air calm. It was a perfect day to hike. Alesha smiled as she grabbed the hiking "go-bag" Zayden had meticulously packed when the weather changed. He even had a repacking list. The man was so organized it sometimes hurt just thinking about it. She made sure that the extra gloves and dry wool socks and extra boot inserts were in each of the children's backpacks, which also included energy bars, lunch, and water.

The hike was invigorating, and Alesha felt alive with the sunshine and cold, clean air. They were in the middle of their hiking group. She let the kids enjoy their walk, laughing when they threw snowballs and raced each other up and down the trail. She had little fear of approaching any wildlife unawares because the noise they were making was surely scaring them off on the next mountain as well.

They had lunch at the top of the trail and glancing at her cell phone, one o'clock meant time to go back. No cell service. She couldn't check to see if Zed was home yet. Well, it would be less time going down but also colder as the afternoon sun waned. She bundled the children, estimating that two hours would give them plenty of time to finish the hike before the sun was gone, and her little charges "fell out" as their father would say.

Less than an hour from the end of the trail, Alesha pointed to a cave she'd played in as a child. "See, there it is again. We aren't far now. When I was a kid, a few years older than Kat, we would play inside. We threw in a flare to make sure no animals were inside first."

"Where did you find the flare?"

"Now, don't tell your daddy I told you this, and don't you do it, but we would grab them off our dads' boats. Only one, though. We always left three in case they needed them for emergencies."

"Can we look inside?" asked Kade.

"Please?" begged Katrina, accompanied by the jumping and chanting Kami.

"Quickly. I'll bring you another time when we can explore in the summer, but just a peek today. Deal? We don't want to disturb any wildlife."

The children readily agreed, wandering into the mouth of the cave while Alli talked to them about what she and her friends would do inside. As she was herding them out to finish their descent, the ground trembled and groaned beneath them. Having lived on the island all her life, she knew that sometimes there were earthquakes. Small ones, nothing large, but you could feel them when you were awake and out like they were now.

"What was that?" asked wide-eyed Kami.

"I think it's an earthquake, but just a small one."

"I thought you couldn't feel the small ones," challenged Kat. Zayden was right; she was way too smart for her age.

"Well, we're outside, so we notice more—"

Kade yelled, "What's that? Thunder now?"

"Of course, n..." Alesha stopped and listened to the roar and watched as clumps of snow and debris fell over them. "Run to the cave, guys. Hurry."

As Alesha made sure the children were behind her, protected by the rocky cavern, she checked that they had the kit bag that Zed had packed. They watched and waited. The thunderous sound filled her with dread. She checked to see what was happening, although she knew without visual confirmation. It was an avalanche. Maybe it wouldn't come this far. She tried to think what Zayden had taught them, wishing with all her heart that he was beside them now.

As she watched, she saw the snow slide was going to catch them, at least a little. Alesha crouched with the children inside the small cave and waited for the inevitable. The twins were painfully silent. Katrina huddling close, waiting. Alli worried the snow would cover the cave entrance as it continued down the pathway. It would go over them as it passed or if they were very lucky, stop before it got to them. She was glad that Zayden had drilled the lessons into her as he practiced. She would never be irritated at his knowledge again. The roar of the fast-moving snow was deafening now, as the children burrowed into her arms for safety. A collective fear rolled off their little trembling bodies.

Suddenly, the earth was moving violently. The air was exploding with unleashed hostility. The entrance to their little safe hideaway was immediately white then dark. The might of the avalanche was receding. As quickly as it came, it was gone.

The world was silent. Breaking into that quiet was subdued sniffles.

The reality of it reminded Alesha that she was not alone. She was responsible for three little children she had grown to love more than life itself. She had to get them involved in their survival to allow them to put this experience in a good light later. If it were only that easy for her. She turned on her first flashlight.

EVER SINCE ALESHA HAD agreed to marry him and he'd gotten the government to buy Alesha's place as the trainee overflow housing, Zed had to pinch himself often. He loved living as a family again, complete with a mother for his children and a woman to love for him. Now, as the newly assembled training team and the other elite forces men who flew in to participate for fun were finishing up, Zed couldn't wait to return home. A residence that had better still be organized when he returned. He and Alesha had quite a few heated conversations to finally get her to agree that "organization" was not a terminal disease to be avoided at all costs. He loved every sizzling and mundane moment of life with Alesha Campbell soon to be Wellesley.

They were just a few miles offshore from the beach next to his house, where they had built a dock for mooring an additional government boat. If there happened to be room to moor his and Alli's personal boats as well, it was a bonus. The team had done an excellent job in giving and receiving training, and he was satisfied that they would be ready to lead their first session in the new year. He was ahead of schedule, but it would be another month before the final inspection and go-ahead to open the center for students.

He was thankful for the group from the Delta team that helped round out the numbers and made this a good training. He'd added and lost a couple of instructors throughout the setup and primary training, but that was to be expected. He hadn't heard from Chopper, but he still held the position open until the final inspection. Zed could almost feel the hot shower, taste the homecooked meal, hear children's excited but contented laughter, and imagine the sweetness of Alli's inner muscles clenching his cock as he brought them both to satisfaction.

Reaching to turn on his phone, he saw his sweetheart had left him a message. He reached to click on the icon to listen when the boat rocked noticeably. The captain was yelling something as he pointed to Wolverine Mountain. A large shelf of snow was sliding down the face of the mountain. *Damn, that's gonna piss Alli off.*

Zed prepared for a grumpy reception to the news. It was her favorite winter hiking spot, but there wouldn't be any hiking there this winter. Finding the trail would be nearly impossible, and then with more winter snowfall to come, the amount of debris that would have to be removed, she'd be lucky if it was able to be used by the end of summer.

Payton, "Brick" who was now Zed's second in command, spoke. "Commander, the captain said he'd been informed that this was an earthquake, setting off that avalanche on the mountain. There's a group of hikers on that trail today, and they aren't sure if everyone has made it off."

He looked at the mountain again. Alli loved hiking that trail, and it looked to be the perfect day for it. And it was a Sunday.

"Hell, Alesha, please don't be on that mountain today, baby."

"Sir?"

Zed's voice held little sign of his anxiety, but it was abundant with authority. "Payton get on the radio and call the Coast Guard. Get us what they know in case we need to coordinate an assist for rescue."

A few minutes later, Zed was speaking with the Coast Guard base commander, formulating a plan. "The Forest Service said they had a group registered for a hike, but it will take a few minutes to check the roster."

"Okay. I'm going to get my guys over to the showers and then regear up should you need us to assist."

"Sounds good. Oh, and Wellesley?"

"Yes?"

"You have a man here who says he's your 'Go Guy,' and should he power up?"

"About damn time. Chopper. Excellent. Tell him to meet me at the house and come with a plan. He can land on the pad behind the trainee quarters."

"Roger that."

Zed turned to his team and filled them in, offering the choice to go home, but they might lose shower time in the transit if they were called back into service, everyone agreed to stay close. To their credit, no one complained, out loud anyway, and they went to the dorm rooms to shower and regroup.

Walking into his front door, Zayden noticed the SUV was gone. His gut cramped. Maybe they went to the store, but it was later than usual. On a typical day, like this one should be, she would have dinner started by now. She said the children needed a routine, and it was the only area of his scheduling she didn't resist. Maybe there was a sports game somewhere that he didn't know about. He checked the whiteboard. Nothing was written, but that didn't mean much. Calendaring at home wasn't her strong suit. They were still working on that.

Zed walked into the bedroom, stripping his gear as he went. He turned on the shower and grabbed his cell phone to call Alesha. Suddenly he longed to hear her voice recounting something from her week with the chatter of the children in the background. Her message, the one he'd forgotten in the excitement of the last few minutes on deck, popped up again, and he clicked to listen.

"Zed, if you're listening to this, then you're home or close. We went hiking up Wolverine Mountain with a group. We'll be home by dark. Love you." His gut churned. He nearly vomited.

Shower forgotten, he switched off the water and dialed the Forest Service direct to get the status on the hikers and prayed his family was safe.

The front door opened, and Zed hurried to identify who it was. He looked up and shook his head as he strode closer. "I've never been so glad to see someone in a long time."

ALESHA LOOKED AT THE children and channeled her best Zayden, daddy to the rescue, voice. "Okay, we have things to set up here, and I'm going to need your help." The children looked at her wide-eyed after the realization that they were trapped inside the cave began to sink in. "Let's look and see what daddy packed us in our 'go bag.'" After all the contents were laid out to be reviewed by everyone, Alli reached for the beacon. "Okay, daddy says it needs to be set to transmit, and it is. Let's put this right by the mouth of the cave as close to the snow as possible."

"We have a pack of starter sticks. We could start a fire and melt the snow," said Kade.

"We don't know how stable everything, especially the snow, is, but we can use our flashlights for light. We each have one, and the go-bag has another, so we'll only use one at a time. Then we will have plenty of light until daddy finds us."

"I want to use mine," said Kami.

"Okay, then I'll turn mine off, and you can use yours first."

"I'm hungry," said Katrina. Alli and Zayden had recently noticed Katrina was a stress eater.

"Okay, well, take one of your snacks out of your packs and eat it but only one. And eat it slowly to help your brain get the message that it has plenty of food. Are you all warm enough?"

The children nodded. The snow was acting as an insulator helping to retain their heat, but that wouldn't last forever. She pulled out her cell phone and tried to use it, but if it didn't work when they were higher up earlier, then it wasn't likely now. Besides, there were too many barriers. Alesha couldn't cry in front of the children, but the urge was almost overwhelming. What if no one knew they were trapped for a while? How long would they have to wait until someone found them? She checked the beacon again. Yep, working. Now they had to wait.

"I know, let's tell fun stories while we wait for someone to come get us. Nothing scary, Kaden."

ZAYDEN WAS THE TEAM point for his guys. It was decided they had enough members for three groups. Brick and Johnny took a team. The search and rescue squad made up another two teams, the forest service another. The Coast Guard and Chopper were on helicopter stand by. They couldn't afford to use them until they were sure things were stable again.

The group had finished the hike. Everyone else was further down the trail or off it when the avalanche occurred. The rescuers had affected an easy removal, but Zayden's family was still up on the path somewhere.

"Where did you see them, Mr. Carlton?"

"I heard them behind me until just before the earthquake hit, and I was about ten minutes from the trailhead."

"Okay, thank you, sir." Zed had to forget it was his family they were looking for and get on with it, but his fear was overwhelming when he thought he might have lost them all.

Mr. Carlton continued. "If anyone can survive this, Alesha can. She had a survival pack, and each of the kids had extra things. We laughed at her, but she said she would be dead if you ever found out she went hiking without the proper supplies. Good thinking, Commander."

Zed nodded. Good. Now, if she remembered what was in there and had her beacon turned to send, they could find her. He turned to Sneakers. "Turn on your beacon to receive, and let's go get my family."

It had been almost an hour, and darkness was descending. The team had been working on the rescue grid, but it was a slow process. Zayden tried to think what Alesha was doing when she realized the avalanche was happening. He'd told her all he knew about how to stay alive and to affect a rescue. Not that Zed expected her to remember it all, but she was a nurse and that part she already knew. The rest, he hoped, would be cued by the supply bag. Alli would have the beacon, so he walked the area with another one on receive. Still no signal. He was going mad with worry, and his temper was short.

Did she have pockets of air? Did she do as he had taught her? They hadn't been yelling across the drifts because there was still a question of stability, but he was making a command decision to fuck that precaution. It had been stable long enough. The rigged floodlights came on, and walking along where they knew the trail had been, he began calling out. The desperation resounded in his voice.

"I HEAR DADDY!" SAID Kami in her half-asleep state.

"Oh, I don't think he's here yet." Alesha's heart raced at the mere mention of Zayden.

"He is, I hear him," Kami insisted.

"Okay, let's all listen carefully." Alli sat up straight.

Alesha thought she heard him. "I hear him too," said an excited Katrina.

"Okay, what did daddy say when you think they are close?"

"Make noise," answered Kaden.

Alesha hesitated, worried about the snow, but it had to be dark now, and they wouldn't find them if not soon.

"Well then, make some noise."

Epilogue

"**M**an, that was the best real-life experience I've ever had while on training. Are you planning on doing that for every finale?" asked one of the Deltas.

Zayden shook his head vehemently. "Hell no. That was a one time shot. I don't think Alli or the kids will volunteer for another round even for a demonstration. But anyone is welcome to bring their own volunteers."

His buddies and new friends laughed as they waved and walked through airport security. The children were at play practice for two more hours. They seemed no worse for the experience, having recounted their version of the story at least a hundred times. Rushing home, Zed walked in the door and was met by nothing but skin. And a glass of wine.

"Alesha, did you check before you met me at the door in this diabolical costume?"

"I did, but I won't always remember, so maybe you need to learn to call and let me know when you are bringing home a playmate from school."

"Oh, I'll call you, alright." His slipped a peaked nipple in his mouth and sucked. Alli squealed.

"Stop, you'll make me spill your last glass of wine. We won't buy any more for a while."

"Really, and why is that?" He asked as he took possession of her mouth, his cock already standing at attention. Ever since the avalanche, the kids had been calling Alli, 'mom.' She was thrilled, and so was he since he couldn't keep his hands off her if they found themselves in the same hemisphere.

Alli pulled away panting and forced the glass into his hand. "Because," her eyes held that mischievous look he'd come to realize made his cock grow hard and needy. "You're going to marry me this Friday."

"We already have that setup, honey, but this is Monday, and what has that got to do with wine?"

"I made arrangements for the kids to get picked up after practice, fed, and then brought home. We have planning to do."

"Planning?" He rubbed his hands up and down her back, detouring to manhandle her scrumptious ass on each round.

"Yep. We are going to plan on how to make another bedroom."

"Why do we need another... Really?" His eyes lit up.

"Yep."

"How?"

"Zayden, how? Really?"

"No, I mean, didn't you start birth control? We talked about it, Alli."

"Well, yes, and no."

"Baby, I might not be up to speed on the latest fashions, but I do know that either you are on birth control or not."

"Yes, well, I didn't want to do any long-term method because if we decided we were ready, then it would be a while before we could try. So, I got the pills."

"Okay."

"Yes, well, taking them effectively required—"

"It required that you be consistent."

"Right."

"If I weren't so excited, I'd blister your ass."

"Promises, promises."

"And you're sure."

She laughed at his question. "Well, the doctor is."

"And you're okay with that?"

She smiled. "Absolutely."

"You know things are going to get tougher for you. I'm a bit anal when it comes to taking care of my pregnant wife."

"I figured." Alli sighed as she accepted his kiss.

"Have I ever told you I do my best planning in bed?"

"I might have heard rumors."

Zayden scooped Alli up, placing another kiss on her lips as he headed for the bedroom. "Then let's go test that rumor."

"Yes, sir."

The End

A NOTE FROM THE AUTHOR

I HOPE YOU'VE ENJOYED SEAL of Refuge, the first story in my Guardians of Refuge romance series. Look for Book 2, The Strategy of Love, coming soon.

There are many ways you can show your support for those who do their part to make this world a better place for all of us. Please remember to appreciate someone who goes out of their way to do you a kindness. When you have the opportunity, a simple thank you goes miles. And don't forget to pay kindness forward. It makes us all better human beings.

Other Romance Books by Alyssa Bailey

Lone Wind Series: Contemporary, spicy Native American

Reclaiming Clover

Lairds, Lords, and Little Ladies: Georgian Historical, spicy

Lord Thayer's Choice

Lord Ashton's Decision

The Black Laird Requires

Lord Kendrick's Obligation

Chase Abbey Series: Regency, Sweet and Spicy, suspense

Lord Barrington's Minx

Becoming Lady Barrington

Lady Caroline's Defiance

His Improper Lady

Safe and Secure Series: Contemporary, suspense, spicy

Saving Sharlee

Saving Jessie

The O'Connor Series: Contemporary, Rancher, Saga, Spicy

Liam & Jocelyn's Story-

Her Sweet Complication

Liam's Lessons

Loving Liam

Ciarán and Katherine's Story

His Gentle Persuasion

Rancher's Creed

Katie Consents

Quinlan and Cheyenne's Story

Quinlan's Quest

Accepting His Way

A Balancing Act

Kelli and Parker's Story

Meeting Her Needs

Kissing Kelli 3) Keeping Kelli

Cián and Molly's Story

In Pursuit of Molly

Freeing Molly

Forever Molly

Clearwater Ranch -Contemporary, Rancher, Spicy

Piper's Plan

Camille's Second Chance

Josie's Refuge (Sept 2020)

Taming Texanna -American Historical, Native American, Spicy

Cowboy Welcome- Contemporary, Spicy

Anthologies

Sweet Town Love

Historical Heroes

Hero to Obey

Cowboy for a Cause

Multi-Author Box Sets (Heat Level Various)

Love, Christmas 2 Movies You Love

Love, Christmas 2 Recipes

Book Bites 11

Christmas Shorts

Irresistible Heroes

Tempting Protectors

Sweet and Sassy Summertime 2

Sexy and Seductive

About the Author

USA Today and #1 International best-selling author, Alyssa Bailey, is a dyed in the wool Texan living amongst the beauty of Southeast Alaska. Along with her husband, she lives where the sky meets the rainforest; the forest meets the mountains that touch the ocean, and the wildlife frolic on land, sea, and air. Humans, the ultimate interlopers, are wedged in where allowed and are properly thankful for the privilege.

Alyssa loves writing realistic romance for the naughty in all of us. As a social worker, a banker, a mother of 11, a "Coastie" military brat and the wife of a retired Army NCO, she takes from her many experiences to write. After scrambling events from her world with her imagination, the fictitious worlds she creates often seem real and draw you in.

She loves writing power exchanges between strong, intelligent, sassy women who are not afraid to make a stand and men confident enough to give his woman space, but Alpha enough to keep her safe despite her choices is a common theme, and of course, there's *always* a happily ever after.

If she can throw a little humor or suspense in her stories, it's even better. Her characters predominately live in Regency England, Ireland, and Scotland amongst lords and ladies, in the Contemporary Realm amongst men and women of the world, and of course, hard-working Cowboys and fiercely romantic Indians.

Read more at alyssabailey.com.